To Lois
Love,

Luis F. Garcia

# *Saving Marina*

By:

Ines Ferrari Garcia

This is a work of fiction. Some of the places mentioned may be real, but all of the characters are strictly a product of the author's imagination, and any resemblance to actual persons, living or dead, is purely coincidental.

This book is dedicated to:

Lisa, Carla and

Carmen

# Saving Marina

*Prologue*

(1958)

"Why? Why did you lie to me? How could you do this to me? How could you sit there and lie to me all these years, and watch me suffer, and let people say those awful things about me when you knew the truth?"

Marina is standing in the middle of the watch tower, crying, shaking, clutching the torn-out pages of her mother's diary.

"I'm suffering too, Marina"

"No. No, you're not. You're not suffering. You don't feel a thing. You're too drunk to feel anything," She sobs. "I hate you! I hate you! I want to die!"

Agnus hears the commotion and goes up the spiral stairs to see what's going on. She knew this was going to happen sooner or later. It was bound to happen. It's been coming for some time now, but just what the fight is about, she has no idea. She enters the third-floor room and sees Cheralena sitting in her rocking chair, stone faced, looking out to sea. A half empty bottle of house brandy on the floor by her side.

Marina is standing over her mother, tears streaming down her face, clutching the torn pages in her fists, her distorted expression, reflected a hundred times in the darkened French doors that frame the room, like a macabre funhouse mirror.

"Oh no", Agnus thinks, "I've angered the gods." She reaches out to take Marina's shoulders in her hands but Marina jerks away.

She drops the papers from her clenched fists and runs out of the room, her bare feet slapping against the hollow metal ship stairs. Agnus bends down and picks up the papers. She smooths them out as best she can and reads them. Her eyes widen to a look of horror as she slowly begins to understand.

She turns to Cheralena; "Is this true?"

"Cheralena just sits there, rocking in her chair, eyes straight ahead, looking out to sea.

"Marina!" Agnus calls, as she hurries down the stairs, as fast as her legs will carry her, papers in hand. Once inside the parlor, she spots the diary sitting next to the old cash box. She carefully places the torn-out pages into the box and runs out the garden gate.

"Marina! Marina! Come back baby girl!" She yells into the night.

Agnus looks up at the clouds moving fast and low; "Storms a' comin'. I've angered the gods for sure," she says to the howling wind. "Sloppy, Sloppy me."

Marina reaches the graveyard. Thunder booms as she runs up and down the rows of headstones in the pouring rain, clutching each one in her hands as she bends over to read the names in the flashing light of the storm.

She runs out of the cemetery and back down the street. Her long white skirt is heavy and wet, and the rain is icy cold on her face. It stings her cheeks as it mixes with her tears. She runs down to the dock, leaning into the screaming wind, barely able to stay on her feet. She slips on the wet boards and lands on her hands and knees at the edge of the dock. Her feet are bleeding from the splinters they just picked up from the old wooden boards, and her hair is plastered to her face from the rain.

"Daddy, oh, Daddy. Please come and get me." She's kneeling at the edge of the dock, hands stretched out to the wind, face pointed to the sky. "Please, Daddy, come and take me away from this place", she screams, unable to hear herself over the sound of the freight train coming up the water toward her.

"Marina! Marina!" Agnus calls after her; "Come back baby girl, come back", she cries.

Marina feels her daddy's strong arms reach down from the sky and embrace her. She looks down into the water and for just an instant sees her reflection, and thinks, "That's not me."

Agnus reaches the dock and hangs onto the lamp post to keep from blowing over in the howling wind. She looks out as the storm lights up the sky. She sees Marina kneeling at the edge of the dock, hands outstretched, face lifted to the sky. Suddenly a waterspout reaches down from the sky and lifts Marina up and holds her there, hanging in midair, like a puppet on a string.

# One

We sit in silence as I look out the window and watch the coastline appear along the edge of the sea below us. A feeling of anticipation washes over me, or is it dread? I think about Carly. I wonder what she's doing right now, my little baby girl all grown up and off to college. Leaving me here lost and looking at the grey abyss which is now my future. No one needs me anymore, and I need to be needed.

Michael reaches over and pats my hand. I look over and smile at him, then turn my attention back to my reflection in the window as the Florida landscape comes up at us and I can make out the familiar landmarks. Michael says he needs me. I wonder. There was a time when we both desperately needed each other, but lately I feel like we don't really have anything in common anymore. He has his life and I have mine. We are just living them side by side.

The plane touches down at Palm Beach International Airport and taxis to the gate. We step outside and the air hits me like a wet blanket. Warm and humid, a typical September morning in South Florida. When we left New York, it was 38 degrees.

We drive down Belvedere Road in silence. Past the gas stations, auto body shops, diners, and the usual stores you see in a blue-collar neighborhood. I'm hoping this weekend is going to be the beginning of something new and good for me. It's been too long since I felt good about my life. I long for something—something meaningful, just for me. I feel as if I've been sitting at a bus stop, waiting, but the bus never comes. I look over at Michael. Poor Michael. He looks worried. He's always worried. I pull down the vanity mirror and look at my hair. Just as I thought; it's a frizzy mess. Two minutes in this humidity and my silky black hair has turned to frizz, oh well. I fish for my lipstick in my Luis Vuitton bag and check my face.

We come to Dixie Highway and head north. I snap the mirror back and close the visor just as we pass an old cemetery on the left. I buried my father down here years ago, in an old cemetery just like that one.

Suddenly I remember the dream I had last night. I dreamt I was in a cemetery. I was walking up and down the rows of headstones, looking for something, but what? Dreams are funny, aren't they? They seem so important at the time we're having them, urgent almost. Then as the day wears on, we toss them aside like abandoned children, forgotten and irrelevant. All my life I have had vivid dreams. Some are reoccurring, some even come true. I've become accustomed to having these strange dreams over the years, and think nothing of them, mostly, but last night's dream is haunting me.

Michael turns east and suddenly the shabby, working-class district gives way to the elegant mansions of the upscale neighborhood of El Cid. The entire neighborhood is six blocks long from north to south, and two blocks wide. Olive Avenue is a picturesque, tree lined street running down the middle, with Flagler Drive to the east, and Dixie Highway to the west. Dixie Highway is the main road, lined with antique shops and restaurants. Flagler Drive is bordered by the water on one side and the homes of the lake block on the other. You either live on the lake block or you live west of Olive, and the prices of the real estate on the two different blocks reflect just how important it is to be on the lake block. We drive around the neighborhood, going up and down streets with Spanish names: Barcelona, Cordova, Granada, Valencia.

"Ah, this must be it!" Michael says, and I snap back to the present moment.

We come to a sprawling property that takes up four lots at the lake end of the block between Granada and Valencia. There is an empty lot on the west side of the house on Valencia, which looks like it used to be a small parking lot that has since grown over with weeds. The house itself faces Flagler Drive and the glistening water beyond. It is two stories tall with a small third story and a widow's walk around the roof line. There is a great sloping lawn and a stone walk leading up to the front gate with two steps spaced every five feet or so. Across the street sits a dilapidated pier that is fenced off. The house is abandoned but must have been grand in its day. Most of the architecture in the neighborhood is some version of Mediterranean Revival, and the homes are all historic—well, as historic as South Florida gets, which means they were probably built in the early 1900s. Before then, there was probably nothing there. This house looks like it could easily have been built along the cliff walk in Newport, Rhode Island. It's a beautiful example of a Mediterranean seaside house, with a wide veranda wrapping around the front and south side.

"Well, it's almost two, we might as well just park and walk around," Michael says. He's out of the car and surveying the land around the building. I'm a little hesitant even though there are no signs of life in the house. I get out of the car and wait by the front gate.

Ten minutes later, and at exactly 2:00 PM, he shows up, driving a banana-yellow Porsche 911 with the top down. He hops out of the car dressed in white slacks, a light blue Tommy Bahama button-down shirt, untucked of course, and light blue suede

Pikolinos with the crest on them. He looks like he just hopped off a yacht.

"Good afternoon. Mrs. Peters, I presume? I'm Stu Stephens."

"Good afternoon, and please call me Teresa," I say. He is so quintessentially Palm Beach; I almost laugh out loud. He's fifty something, with wavy blonde hair, and I would swear he gets his eyebrows done.

"Allow me to present to you Villa Cheralena," he continues with a bow, as if he's introducing a grand dame at a cocktail reception. And with that he opens the front gate.

We proceed up the walk to the stone steps that lead to the wide veranda, and the massive, carved mahogany front doors. I think about calling out for Michael, but realize he is already behind us, and coming towards the door. Michael puts his hand out to shake Stu's, and I swear I see Stu actually click his heels when he takes Michael's hand.

"Stu Stephens, at your service."

Oh, my God, is this guy for real? Michael steals a quick glance at me behind Stu's back and raises his eyebrows as if to ask the question, and we all continue into the house.

"She was built in 1925 by a wealthy businessman named Johnny Cotton. She was a Grande Dame in her day. Cotton purchased the land from the wealthy socialite Jay Phipps, who had purchased the entire El Cid neighborhood from a pineapple farmer. Cotton named her Villa Cheralena for his wife, and they operated it as a hotel during the early 1900s."

He sweeps his arm into the space and announces, "The ballroom is to the left. The dining room to the right, the kitchen and maid's quarters are in the back of the house, and there are ten en-suite bedrooms upstairs, plus the master suite and third-floor observation room. Mr. Cotton died during the war, and Mrs. Cotton never remarried. She stayed on and ran the Hotel as a boarding house for the soldiers returning from the war. After their only daughter died, Mrs. Cotton closed the boarding house, along with most of the upstairs rooms, and lived here alone until she died last year at the age of ninety and left the property to her church. The property is being sold "as is" for one point two mil, along with the original Schonbek crystal chandeliers."

"Does that also include the pier across the street?" Michael asks.

"You mean the old marina? Why, yes, yes it does," he replies.

I think it's odd that Stu thinks to include the chandeliers in his verbal presentation and not the marina, as if the chandeliers are more valuable.

"And now, if there are no more questions, I'll let you two look around." And with that he pulls out his cell phone, turns his back to us, and starts making phone calls.

I'm not sure if Stu just wants to leave us alone, or if his other clients on the phone are more important. Maybe he thinks we're just wasting his time, and he'll never sell us this old house. Maybe he's right.

We step into the ballroom, which takes up the entire left wing of the house. Ten-foot-high arched French doors lead out onto the veranda, facing Flagler Drive and the water just beyond. I look up. Two huge pecky cypress beams break up the eighteen-foot-high plaster ceiling into three sections. Each section is ornately carved and painted with a blue sky and white puffy clouds. There are images of cherubs floating around the clouds playing harps. In the center of each section is a round, heavily carved plaster medallion, with one of the glimmering crystal Schonbek chandeliers hanging down from a velvet-slip-covered chain. The chandeliers are sparkling in the sunlight, throwing rainbow-colored prisms onto the black and white diamond-patterned marble floor. Stu obviously likes those chandeliers more than the house itself, since only they are kept dusted and sparkling clean.

Floating out from the back wall of the ballroom is a grand spiral staircase with black marble treads and white marble risers. A black iron handrail, right out of *"Gone with the Wind."* leads up to the second floor and the ten guestrooms. Someone must have opened a window because I suddenly feel a breeze and I hear a wind chime in the distance. I'm light-headed and a little dizzy. I have a feeling I can't quite put my finger on, like I've been here before.

We decide to save the upstairs for later and walk back through the foyer and into the dining room.

This room is smaller and more intimate, but still huge by anyone's standards, with four arched French doors on the east side of the house that match the ones in the ballroom. There are wide plank hardwood floors covered with an enormous, old Persian rug filling up most of the space. The walls are paneled and painted an antique white, and there is a great big fireplace with a mantel along the north wall. From the center of the tongue-and-groove pecky cypress ceiling hangs yet another Schonbek chandelier. The light fixtures alone are worth a fortune. Maybe they are more valuable than the pier after all.

Just outside the dining room, leading to the kitchen and under the back stair is a small powder room in total need of repair. Beyond are the kitchen and maid's room. The maid's room is not ornately decorated like the other rooms of the house, but it will make a good office. The kitchen, which was probably updated in the 1960s, needs to be totally gutted, but it's a good size, taking up most of the back-center portion of the house.

We walk up the back stair to the master suite, which is enormous. They just didn't build master bedrooms like this in the early 1900s. The suite consists of a large sitting room, the bedroom itself, a master bath and two walk-in closets. The bedroom looks out to the east and north, a perfect exposure for a master bedroom. Right outside the suite, at the landing of the back stair, is a metal ship's spiral stair that leads up to the third-floor observation room.

The observation room is small, with French doors all around leading out to the widow's walk. Standing there, looking out of those French doors at the panoramic view of the entire neighborhood, Palm Beach Island, and the ocean beyond, I suddenly realize I have just fallen in love with this house. It feels like home.

Meanwhile, I can tell Michael is thinking just how bad a shape the house is in. Although it has good bones, most of the house needs to be either refinished or demolished and rebuilt altogether. I don't think he notices what I see, but then he never does.

Michael walks back down the spiral stair and then down the back stair, with me following on his heels like the dutiful wife. Then we walk back around to the grand stair and ascend to the guest quarters. We walk around the second floor for a while. We haven't said two words to each other the entire time, both of us deep in our own thoughts. Michael knocks on a few doors, checks out the damage to the original hardwood floors, examines the heavy plaster walls and the windows that will all need replacing, and heads back downstairs toward the kitchen.

He opens the electrical box and shakes his head.

"This place is a fire hazard, a real tinder box just waiting to go up in flames," he says. He wonders aloud if the electric even works when Stu suddenly appears out of nowhere and proceeds to tell us that the electric does, in fact, still work, and not only that, but that most of the other historical houses in El Cid still have their original cloth wiring as well.

"Most people just change out the box and leave the wiring intact," Stu says.

Michael is about to thank him for his time and get the hell out of here. I have to think fast.

"I love it, honey. Let's buy it," I whisper.

"What? Are you crazy? It will take a year, and a million dollars just to make this place livable again!"

I realize that I very well may be crazy, but an overwhelming feeling comes over me—I just have to have this house.

"I think I can do it for a half to three quarters. Please, let's do it?" I whisper.

Michael turns and walks over to Stu, puts his hand out and says, "Thank you very much for your time, Mr. Stephens, we'll be in touch."

"The church is very motivated to get it off their books," he says, and by the look on Michael's face I can tell he doesn't doubt him for a minute.

We walk out and say our goodbyes at the front door.

Stu gives Michael his card and says, "Feel free to call me with any questions you may have."

"Thank you," replies Michael. "We're just going to check out the yard and the pool. We'll be in touch."

We walk around the back toward the pool, as Stu hops back into his overpriced yellow sports car and zooms away.

"Are you crazy?" Michael asks again. "What are you thinking? I thought you didn't want to do any major renovations?"

"Well, maybe I changed my mind," I say. I really don't know what I'm thinking as I continue walking around the pool, trying to avoid his eyes. I'm not going to let him see my weakness.

"Do you know what you're saying? This isn't just a redecorating job. This is a major renovation we're talking about."

I hate it when he talks down to me like that. Like I don't know it's a major renovation because I'm just a decorator and he's Mr. Architect, Mr. Know-it-all. I've been here before with him. I hold my ground and show no emotion. It's a delicate dance we perform in this marriage. Sometimes it feels like a competition, sometimes I'm carrying him, and sometimes we're walking alone. And sometimes I feel like I'm pushing a heavy sack of potatoes up a steep hill. He's always so negative, the glass half empty. It's all fear based; I know. And I also know I can usually make him come around to my way of thinking, but sometimes it's hard work. It's hard work getting through that wall of his, that wall of perfection, and safety. He calls me Pollyanna, but lately I don't feel like Pollyanna. I've lost that positive thinking somewhere and I don't know where to find it again. Maybe this house, maybe.

"You know I've been wanting to do this for a long time, right? This is my dream, Michael - to renovate an old house and turn it into a bed and breakfast. And this house, this house seems so right, like it's been just waiting for me, like it was meant to be."

"Yes, but—"

"Just hear me out. Maybe I can quit my job and oversee the renovations. I can stay at the Breakers, and you can come down on the weekends. We'll have this place up and running in six months or less. Then you can finally retire, and we can run the bed and breakfast together, just the two of us, just like we planned."

"Are you out of your mind? You want to handle the entire process by yourself? And live at the Breakers? Now I know you're crazy," he says.

I can see his reflection staring into the pool. What happened to the man I married so long ago? Would that Michael be afraid to take on such a project? Would that Michael hesitate to jump on this for even an instant?

"Well, maybe you're right. I might have to find a more suitable place to stay, but look, this house is magnificent, and the price is so cheap. Even if we don't open it up as a bed and breakfast. Say we just renovate it and flip it? We could make a million dollars or more on this property! I wonder why no one else has picked it up?"

"Maybe because it's a dump?" Michael says under his breath.

But I don't take the bait. I don't want to fight. I pretend not to hear him. I'm busy thinking about getting out from under my hectic job and doing something creative again, just for me. Work has been so stressful, and these headaches I've been getting are starting to worry me.

"I think it would be good for me", I say. "I would love to fix up this old house and turn it into my dream—*our* dream retirement."

But Michael can't seem to get past the part about me living down in Florida all alone. "But all alone? I don't know if I can let you do that."

"Sure, you can. You know I'm more than capable, and you know that one of us needs to keep their job for the security and the benefits during the renovation process. As soon as it's looking close to completion, you can give your notice and hop on a flight. Whaddya say?" I squeeze his arm.

We're still walking around the pool, which needs much work, but is actually quite stunning, or used to be. It's a large rectangle running north to south with a simple two-foot-wide coral stone edge around it, surrounded by grass.

"I like the way they did pools in those days—no big concrete decks, just a grassy lawn. It's so very natural and serene looking. I can imagine sputter fountains flanking the long sides of the pool, with water arching into it. We could also add a jacuzzi at the north end of the—"

Just then I see a fox run from under a bush and climb under the overgrown bougainvillea in the corner of the yard. I stop speaking mid-sentence.

"Did you see that?" I ask.

"What?"

"I think I just saw a fox", I say

"You're imagining things. There are no foxes around here. It was probably just a big cat", Michael says without showing much interest.

"With a red, bushy tail?"

"You're crazy, honey. There are no foxes in this area", he says, this time with authority.

19

How the hell does he know that? I walk over to where I saw the fox run, in the corner of the yard, and Michael follows me. There is a wall running perpendicular from the house and then north to the end of the property line. In the middle of the north side is a wrought iron gate all covered in creeping fig.

"Well, what do we have here?" Michael asks out loud as he rips away some vines and peers through the gate. He tries to open it, but it's locked.

I walk over and lean in to see what he's looking at and Michael holds back the little red vines with tiny green leaves, like a curtain. I peer through the opening into a garden. Was I seeing things or was that really a fox?

There is a wall, probably eight feet high, interspersed with three stone pilasters every five feet or so, surrounding a garden. The wall is entirely covered in creeping fig, badly in need of a trim. There is a fountain to the left that has long since dried up. A Greek goddess stands guard in a flowy stone robe, her head adorned with a crown of acanthus leaves. She's tipping her stone urn down toward the fountain, as if she is perpetually filling it with water. Yellow butterflies (there are dozens of them) are playing with the bumble bees, buzzing in and around the overgrown bougainvillea in full magenta bloom. Stone benches, all covered in moss, sit against the green wall in between the stone pilasters. And leggy blue wildflowers, having seen better days, are growing in stone pots, scattered all around. There's a little stone plaque lying on the ground in the far corner of the garden. With the sun's rays slanting through the gate, the garden looks like a Thomas Kinkade painting, a private little piece of heaven that time has forgotten.

"It's a secret garden," I whisper in awe. Wind chimes tinkle in the corner.

"Let's go around to the other side and take a look," Michael says.

Should I mention the fox again? We walk around the front of the house to the north side, and west to the back. Did I really see a fox after all? I'm starting to doubt it. Maybe it really was just a big cat. All along the north side is the same privacy wall, about eight feet tall, all covered in creeping fig. In the middle of the wall hangs a small marble plaque that reads, "Villa Cheralena."

"Come on, let's call Stu and put an offer down," I plead, getting back to the subject at hand.

"I don't know, honey. Let's think about it. We still have two more properties to see."

There he goes again, treating me like a little child. Talking down to me in that condescending voice of his. He thinks he can ·

close the subject just like that. But two can play at this game. I want this house. With or without the fox, I want this house.

"I don't need to see any other properties. This is the one I want. It's this or nothing." I say in my most stubborn voice.

"Well, let's think about it anyway. Tomorrow's Saturday and we're here for two more days. Why don't we sleep on it, and if you still feel the same way tomorrow, we'll call him and come back and take a second look. I don't think it's going anywhere since it's been up for six months already, and it doesn't look like anyone is banging down the doors to buy it."

He's softening up. I got him right where I want him. I soften my stance in return.

"Deal," I say with a big smile, and I turn around and give him a big hug and kiss. This time Michael succumbs to the sparkle in my eyes and lets himself relax into my arms.

We stand there like that for a while, holding on to each other. The sweet scent of honeysuckle is riding on the warm breeze, the wind chimes are singing. I am happy to be away from the cold winter in the city, and away from the pressures of work. And I can tell Michael's happy just to be holding me in his arms.

Suddenly I catch a glimpse of something out of the corner of my eye. I look again, but there is nothing there. The wind whispers something in my ear, a distant memory of an old friend.

# TWO

We drive back to the hotel in silence, each caught up in our own thoughts. We turn onto a long, winding drive flanked by royal palms on either side like soldiers standing guard in a parade. Suddenly a Mediterranean castle breaks into view.

The Breakers was built in the early 1900s by none other than Henry Flagler, the great American industrialist, and founder of the Florida East Coast Railway. The hotel is still run as a family business and it shows. No detail is left unattended, no request unfulfilled. We walk through the opulent lobby to the front desk to check in. Our room is ready, so we head upstairs. Michael makes small talk with the bellhop and then tips him and closes the door. I look out through the French doors to the ocean. The melancholy along with the headache of yesterday have disappeared.

There's a little pink restaurant with a painted green door that sits smack in the middle of Worth Avenue, called Ta-boo. Ta-boo is *the* place to be seen in Palm Beach. It's been a Palm Beach institution since its opening in 1941. Everybody who is anybody has dined at Ta-boo over the years, including Frank Sinatra and the Kennedys.

I'm wearing a little black off-the-shoulder crepe dress and black Tory Burch sandals that I bought at the gift shop at the Breakers. I glide into the restaurant as if in a dream as Michael holds the door open for me. I have my hair up in a classic French twist and I'm wearing the string of pearls around my neck that Michael gave me for our wedding anniversary last year. Although it is still off-season for Palm Beach and the place is nearly empty, the hostess looks up and smiles, and asks if we have reservations.

"Yes, Michael Peters."

"Very good, Mr. Peters. Right this way, please." And she shows us to a table right in front of the window near the entrance. "Will this be ok?"

"It's fine," Michael says as he pulls the chair out for me.

"It's perfect," I say with a smile.

The dining room is elegantly decorated with animal prints on the walls and bold black and white stripes on the upholstered chairs. There's a cozy fireplace in the middle of the main room, but I like it better by the window. Here I can see the people as they walk by, and I'm hoping to spot a famous island regular like Rod Stewart. The waiter arrives instantly and hands us menus and we order drinks.

"Hey, look at this." I point to the anecdotes on the back of the menu. "It says that this restaurant used to have a roll-away roof, so you could dine under the stars at night."

"It also says that the Germans used to sneak ashore and come here for cocktails during World War II," Michael muses.

There are many stories about the German U-boats off the coast of Florida during the war. The local fishermen and yachtsmen from Palm Beach would patrol the waters just off the island, looking for them. Ernest Hemmingway was among them. He would take his notorious boat *Pilar* out, armed with hand grenades and a couple of rifles. No doubt he and his buddies would go drinking afterward on such nights.

"The legend says the captain of the U-boat would come to Ta-boo and sit at this very bar and drink with the locals," he continues.

"Wow, I wonder if they knew they were drinking with the Germans," I ponder as I sip my gin and tonic. "Florida might not have a long history compared to the northeast, but it certainly has an interesting one."

"My dad was on a German U-boat during the war," I say. "I remember him telling me the story of when he was in the Italian navy fighting against the U.S. They were patrolling the Florida coast, and they would surface at night and row ashore in rubber inflatables. They would go to the brothels on the mainland, and drink and party until the wee hours of the morning. Then they would hop in their little boats and row back to the submarine before the sun came up. That's how he got captured during the war. He stayed too long in the brothel one night, and when he tried go back to his boat, they were waiting for him on the dock. They shipped him off to prison camp in Jacksonville."

"Wow."

"He painted a portrait of the warden while he was in that prison. He still had the pencil sketch, and a letter from the warden thanking him for the painting when he died. After they beheaded Mussolini and dragged him through the streets of Italy, the US Army came and asked my father, along with the other prisoners of war, if they were ready to switch sides and fight with the Americans. The Army offered him a full pardon and the chance to be an American citizen. Naturally, he said yes. He stayed in the US Army for another year providing intelligence, and when the war was over, he got an honorable discharge. They even played "Taps" at his funeral when he died. He told my mom he wanted to be buried in Florida. It was the first US soil he had ever put his feet on, and it felt like home to him. He used to say that his true love was in the waters off South Florida. He's buried around here somewhere. I don't remember where, though. I don't remember much about his funeral."

"You weren't that close to you father, were you?"

"No, not really. He left when I was just six years old."

"He was an architect, wasn't he?"

"Yes, just like you, my love."

"So, you married your father, did you?"

"Well, I wouldn't know that. I never really got to know anything about his work, except that I thought it was mysterious and marvelous to be able to color for a living. When I was a little girl, I used to sneak into his studio when he wasn't home and marvel at all his supplies. Drafting tools and rolls of trash paper, colored pencils and pastels. The studio smelled of cigarettes and turpentine. His latest drawings would be out on his drafting table. A colored rendering of a restaurant he was designing, or the old-fashioned blueprints of some office building in New York. I never stayed long though, and I certainly never touched anything for fear of getting him upset. He had a terrible temper, and I spent most of my early years walking on eggshells, or just trying to stay out of his way."

"Wow, too bad." Michael has never heard Teresa speak about her father before and he wonders why this is coming up now, but he's genuinely interested in hearing about him. He wishes he could have gotten to know him better while he was still alive. And he wishes Teresa could have had a better relationship with her father. In any case, he's just happy to be here with her tonight, just sitting here, enjoying each other's company, like they are on a date. Teresa looks radiant tonight, just like she did when they were first dating. Before they got married, and before they had Carly.

"What is it?" I ask. He's staring at me with a funny look on his face now.

"Nothing. I'm just enjoying having my wife back, and I'm enjoying how beautiful you look tonight."

I feel myself blush.

"Luckily, he left us when I was six," I continue. "I say luckily because it was getting so bad toward the end. They would fight every night. I remember falling asleep to them fighting, like some kind of sick lullaby. And when it suddenly got quiet, I would get really scared, because I thought he might have killed her."

"Wow, that's really sad."

I wonder why this is coming up all of a sudden. Maybe being in Florida has sparked some memories for me.

"Somehow though, I always loved my father, or the idea of him anyway. I never saw much of him after he left my mother and me. He just packed up his things one day and left. My mother never told me what happened, and she never talked about my father again. He came back to visit a couple of times, but they were usually brief and stressful visits."

I try not to think about it anymore. The past is a dark, cloudy place. Anyway, it is over and done with. I look out the window at an elderly couple passing by. They are walking hand in hand. I wonder if Michael and I will last that long. I've never really had much confidence in the merits of marriage. And I certainly have never trusted men. I wonder why I'm feeling this way tonight, just when things are going so well with Michael. I think back to the first time we met twenty-four years ago.

It was my first day at Princeton. I walked into the design studio late one afternoon and there he was, leaning over a drafting table with his hands in his hair, looking like he was concentrating hard on something important. I was in my freshmen year and feeling very inadequate, knowing deep down that I didn't belong there. I was in over my head going to Princeton, but I had gotten in with a full scholarship. I had gathered that the college needed to fill a quota of poor white girls from broken homes in New Jersey.

When I walked into that studio, he raised his head and smiled and said hello. Right then and there a little voice in my head said, "There's the man you're going to marry."

We didn't start dating seriously until after graduation. Although we were very close friends, Michael felt he didn't need the distraction of a girlfriend while he was in school. That was just like him. So disciplined, so grown up, so talented and focused.

We got married soon after graduation. Funny thing about my life—I waited so long for him to love me and then suddenly it happened so quickly. Once he told me he loved me, we were engaged and then we were married, just like that. And then we had Carly, and my whole life changed again.

We go back to the hotel and sneak into the pool for a late-night swim. The moon is full, and the pool water is just as warm as the air. Michael brings a bottle of champagne and two glasses down from the hotel room, and we sip champagne and lounge by the pool until midnight. Then we go for a short stroll along the beach before heading back to the room.

We go up to the room around one and make love until we fall asleep in each other's arms. As I drift off to sleep, I already know that Michael's answer in the morning will be yes, and that we will be buying that old house. I smile to myself as I watch the moonlight throw shadows into the room through the opening in the drapery.

That night I have a strange dream:

*I slip out of the garden gate and walk west in the dead of night. The ground is cool and damp under my bare feet and my long white skirt, heavy with mud, is trailing on the wet ground. Tears are flowing freely down my cheeks and my heart is pounding. The moon is full and round. It throws its light onto the coconut palms, casting shadows all around me, as the fronds sway restlessly in the warm night air. I can smell the sweet scent of night jasmine. I walk faster now, my eyes cast down as the ominous shadows chase me down the street. I know this street. I know all the houses that line this street, their windows darkened now, their occupants fast asleep. The Spanish Mediterranean painted the color of mangoes ripe from the sun, with arched windows trimmed in brown. The fountain in the front, crying softly like a child from some long-ago memory. The white Italian Villa, sprawled atop a perfectly manicured lawn, adorned with planters overflowing with frangipani, jacaranda, and blood lily in every color. The old English Tudor standing straight and tall, with a pair of Black Labrador statues that sit proudly on great stone pillars and guard the brick driveway.*

*I reach the main road and head south. I walk along the iron fence that surrounds the graveyard. I pass through the black iron archway and enter the cemetery. I'm walking up and down the rows looking for something, searching.*

## Saving Marina

*The moonlight plays with my shadow along the headstones like a silent flicker film at a carnival. But unlike those old films at the carnival, this is not a funny story. No, this story is a heartbreak. Sorrowful and lonely.*

## THREE

Agnus walks onto the beach dressed in white gauze pants and a white tank top. Her hair is piled high in a white head scarf and her black skin glows in the moonlight. She's thin and fit for an old woman, and she carries a large shell shaped bowl full of fruit down to the water's edge.

The ocean is rough for early September, but the wind is still calm as the sun hasn't shown its early morning color yet.

Agnus places the bowl of fruit down on the sand; watermelon, pineapples, grapes, and bananas. She proceeds to make a circle around the bowl with seven pennies, taking extra care not to be sloppy in her prayers today. She fingers the necklace of blue and crystal beads that hangs around her neck. Standing behind the offering, she faces the ocean as she recites her prayer to Yemaya, the Mother Goddess, who rules over the oceans, the moon, women & children, fisherman & sailors, witches & secrets.

She repeats the prayer for each bead; seven crystal, seven blue, one crystal, one blue, and again seven times.

"Hail Mary, full of grace

Enlightenment is in thee.

Blessed are thee among women.

Blessed is the fruit of thy womb.

Holy Mary, mother of us all,

Bless us mortals now and

Throughout our life."

The wind picks up as the hot pink rays of the sun start to peek out from the horizon. Agnus spreads her arms wide as the trail of her head scarf whips in the wind. She says her final "Amen". Then she sits down cross-legged in the sand and asks Yemaya for protection and safety, just as she has done every Saturday since she was a little girl. She thanks Yemaya, leaves the offering on the beach and heads home just as the sun rises over the sea. She can feel the Mother Goddess smiling down on her as she walks over the bridge to the mainland, and she knows Yemaya is pleased. But today Agnus feels something else as well. Something's coming; she can sense it. She hopes it's good, but in any case, she knows she'll have her work cut out for her.

FOUR

I wake up exhausted at nine, which is late for me, even for a Saturday. Michael is already up and dressed in his bathing suit. He looks bothered and distant, but I try not to notice.

"Why don't you throw on your suit and we can go down for breakfast and a swim?" he asks, as he brushes a distracted kiss against my cheek. Neither one of us tries to make eye contact. What happened to last night? We're back to being polite strangers again.

"Ok, let me just wake up a minute," I say. My head is pounding. What was that dream? Was I really walking through a graveyard? It seemed so real. What was I looking for?

"It's going to be another hot one." Michael says as we exit the elevator and head over to the pool.

We sit at a table in the shade and order coffee and breakfast. The yogurt parfait for me and the blueberry muffin for Michael.

"Look at your feet! They're black!" Michael comments.

I look down at my feet in my new Tory Burch sandals. He is such a clean freak. I can't believe he's commenting on my feet, when he's the one who wanted to go for a walk on the beach last night at midnight. I hope it's tar or something from the sand, instead of the black mud from the cemetery. But it couldn't be, could it?

"I love these shoes, they're so comfortable. I'd hate to have to throw them away. They just don't make things like they used to," I reply, trying to sound casual.

"Anyway, I've decided," I say, taking a risk and changing the subject, "I'm going to call that Stu and tell him we want the house."

"No, don't do that," Michael says. "Just tell him we want to go back and have another look."

"Are you having second thoughts?" I ask, disappointed. I really want that house. I know it's silly, but I feel a connection to it I can't quite explain.

"No, I just don't want him thinking we're desperate to have it or anything. I want to be able to bargain the price down a little bit."

"Ok, smart move," I say, and I pull out my phone and dial the realtor's number. He picks up after one ring.

"Stu Stephens, here." So prompt, so professional.

"Hi Mr. Stephens. This is Mrs. Peters. My husband and I would like to take another look at that house in El Cid today, if you can find the time. We also have some questions," I add, hoping this sounds like we're interested, but doubtful about purchasing.

"I can meet you there in an hour," he says.

Wow, prompt indeed. "Let's make it two," I say. We agree to the time, exchange pleasantries and hang up. "We're meeting him there in two hours."

"Great," says Michael, distracted now, watching last nights' hockey game on the TV by the bar. The Caps beat the Rangers again.

As we go back up to the room to shower and get dressed, I toy with the idea of telling Michael about the dream I had last night, but in the end, decide against it.

We pull up to the house exactly two hours later and Stu pulls in right after us. He must have been parked just down the street, watching us or something. Too much of a coincidence.

"Good afternoon, Mr. and Mrs. Peters.," he says, opening the door. He hands Michael some paperwork and says, "I've taken the liberty of bringing the owner's disclosure documents with me, along with the neighborhood association paperwork, and Historical Board papers. You see, this house, as well as the entire neighborhood, is listed on the National Registry of Historic

Landmarks. If you're going to do any renovations, you must first be approved by the board. But don't worry, it's easy. I live right down the street."

Ah, that explains it. He *was* watching us pull up.

"I did my own house a few years ago. They'll let you do pretty much anything you want, except change the outside. They want you to keep the same look. But you can gut the entire inside of the house if you want, and even add on to the back, although I doubt you'll want to do that. The house is plenty big enough."

Boy, this guy is a slick, fast talker. I don't remember him behaving this way yesterday.

We're standing in the kitchen now, and Michael is leaning on the counter looking over the documents. I'm standing beside him looking out the window at the pool and the yard beyond. A yellow butterfly is fluttering its wings just outside the window and it catches my eye.

"I've also taken the liberty of bringing with me a blank contract for purchase. All you have to do is fill in the offering price here and sign here, and…."

Wow, who told him we were interested? Does he have us bugged as well?

"I can tell you the church is willing to go down a couple of hundred at the most, but they won't take anything under seven figures."

"We'll offer a million dollars, and no more," Michael says, without even consulting me! I'm ready to put up a fight, give him a dirty look, or at least nudge him; we never even talked about a price. Why does he always make me feel so insignificant? But then I remember the secret garden around the back.

"Mr. Stephens," I say, "is there a private garden that leads out from the dining room or something? I noticed a privacy wall around that part of the yard yesterday."

"Oh, yes, that," he says. "The old lady used to grow vegetables there and the critters were intent on eating her crops, so I guess she put up a wall. There is a gate out back, but I think it's locked. I don't believe there is a way to enter the garden from the house."

I wonder if I should ask him about the fox but decide to let it go. It is clear Stu has no intention of showing us the garden, and Michael does not seem all that interested in it at the moment, either. He is busy signing the paperwork.

"When is the soonest we can close?" he asks. "We will have cash."

"Oh, well, a cash deal. In that case, we can close as soon as you like."

"Let's say October 30th then," says Michael, checking his calendar on his cell phone. "That's a Thursday."

"Perfect," says Stu, suddenly looking more relaxed and like he is our best friend.

Michael slides the contract over to me to sign, and Stu informs us that he will fax a copy to the hotel. He also gives Michael the names of several contractors in the area in case we're interested. What a salesman. I hesitate for just a moment before signing my name on the line above *Buyer # 2* and glance out the window to see the yellow butterfly again, fluttering in little zig-zag patterns, like a tiny sky writer trying to portray some message. Is it telling me to sign or not to sign? I hesitate for just another moment, but then sign the contract and hand it over to Stu, who promptly stuffs it in his folder, clicks his heels and nods. Then he turns and walks toward the front door.

"Wow, that happened fast!" I say to Michael, making sure Stu can't hear me.

Michael is already making notes with pen and paper and drawing sketches for the renovation.

"We'd like to stay around for a while and make a few notes, take a few pictures, if you don't mind," Michael tells Stu.

"Of course, take your time. I'm right down the street. Just give me a call when you're finished, and I'll come and lock up."

I suddenly feel invisible.

Stu hops back into his car like he just won the lottery and speeds away.

Michael has closed the door after Stu and is already in the great room sketching the window wall. As I walk into the great room after Michael, I see a shadow move across the floor.

"There's not much we have to do, really. Of course, we have to get all new impact windows, get these marble floors refinished, and the upstairs floors sanded and stained, maybe just paint the handrail on the stair, but this heavy plaster, it has to go."

I'm not sure if he's talking to me or himself, as I wasn't even in the room yet when he started his sentence. Why is he suddenly so interested? This is my project, after all.

The floor in the ballroom is a beautiful black and white diamond-patterned marble, and the handrail on the marble grand stair is a decorative iron scroll. There's that shadow again! It looks like the reflection of someone gliding up the stairs in a long dress. It must be the sunlight playing off the chandeliers.

"Not much to do? Are you kidding? There isn't even any air conditioning! I'm going to have my work cut out for me." Is this buyer's remorse I'm feeling already?

"Ah, that's the beauty of these old houses. You really don't need air, you see. If you open the windows on the top floors and these French doors downstairs," he says, pointing to the windows he is currently sketching, "it acts as an air flume. The breeze comes in off the water and is pulled up the stairs and out the upper windows. Natural air conditioning!"

He doesn't seem to be talking to me, or even noticing me. Suddenly I feel like I'm suffocating, I need some air.

"Of course, we will install the real thing. There's plenty of height in the ceilings upstairs for duct work, and the handler can go in one of the closets. The house has a crawl space below and it actually breathes, like a living thing. What a beauty."

I recognize this rambling of his now. He does this whenever he's excited. I sit down on the grand stair; I've got to catch my breath a minute.

"We can add another handler down here and run our duct under the house for the first floor. We'll also have to change the entire electrical system. But other than that…" he trails off, making more notes in his pad.

Michael walks over and shows me his pad. He has sketched the entire great room in a three-point perspective. The sketch shows the French doors open, with sheer curtains blowing into the room on some invisible breeze. It looks so romantic; I want to cry. That's exactly how I envisioned this room. How can he know me so well? I can almost feel the warm breeze on my face.

"Here," he says, closing the sketch pad and handing me the smart end of the tape measure, "let's get some as-builts down on paper so I can start the drawings and get some bids before we close."

And with that, we're off and running. The rest of the weekend is a blur. No more romantic dinners by the water, no more lovemaking. Michael is all up in his head now, planning.

I know I should be, too. At least I should be excited, but something inside me is not liking the way this is going. Suddenly, I feel overwhelmed, like I'm in over my head. Plus, I'm worried about going home and giving my notice at work. It's fine to talk about it but having to actually quit my job won't be easy for me. I've been there for so long, I'm afraid I'm going to miss it. But I keep my mouth shut and decide to try, for Michael's sake, to take an interest in what he's saying. After all, wasn't this all my idea? Isn't this exactly what I wanted when we came down here in the first place? It's all just happening too fast, that's all. I know I'll feel better about it in the morning, once I have some time to get used to the idea.

That night, I'm lying in bed, asleep, dreaming:

*I'm pouring drinks for table number twenty-five, and all the while I'm thinking, "I'm having my Waitress Dream." It's a busy night and the place is packed. It's a dirty little diner and the food is lousy here; I don't even know why I'm working here. I hate the cook, and I hate my boss. They are both screaming at me now to pick up.*

*"Pick up! Pick up! Hot food!" they are yelling, but I don't care.*

*I have to get these drinks to table number twenty-five. I finish pouring red wine into three dirty glasses, and I carry my tray over to the crowded dining room. There are people everywhere, standing next to the crowded tables, waiting to sit down and order. There are other people already sitting at the tables, waving their hands at me to signal that they have been ready to order for too long, and they are getting impatient. I'm sweating. My head is pounding. I have to get to table number twenty-five, but I can't find it! I'm walking up and down the rows of tables looking for a familiar face. Who ordered these drinks? I can't recognize anyone, and I can't remember what the people looked like who ordered this wine.*

*Suddenly I walk straight into the back of a girl and the glasses of red wine tumble off my tray. She turns around and looks right into my eyes. She is about nineteen years old and she's dressed all in white. She looks vaguely familiar, like I should know who she is, but I can't place the face. There is red wine all over her white clothes, and there is red wine all over me as well. Suddenly the wine turns to blood, and the restaurant is on fire!*

I wake up in a sweat and my head is pounding. That stress dream—I recognize it. I've had it before. I have to go to the doctors and see if I can get some sleeping pills or something. If this is menopause, and I have to suffer these night sweats and headaches for the next couple of years, I don't think I can do this without some help. I lie in bed, awake for the rest of the night.

# FIVE

"Did ya hear?" The door slams and the bells ring as they crash onto the blue painted doorframe of the little antique shop, Lost Treasures.

Agnus walks out from the back room. She is wearing a long, sleeveless, black dress made of cotton gauze and a colorful silk head scarf tied in the front at her forehead. Her signature gold hoop earrings touch her collar bone and she's taken to wearing the blue and crystal beads every day lately for extra protection.

"Well, hello, Daisy." She says.

"Don't you give me that *hello, Daisy*. I tell you I got news, bad news."

"Come sit down, child, and have some tea." she says. She motions to the red velvet settee placed strategically at the center of the small shop, so people can sit and feel at home, while they look around.

There are end tables with Tiffany lamps at each side of the settee and a coffee table in front, piled high with books and candles and other small decorative objects. Behind the settee is a large sofa table filled with shell-shaped bowls holding beaded bracelets and necklaces not unlike the one Agnus is wearing. Also, on that table are more books; books on decorating and architecture, and the history of Palm Beach and the surrounding areas, books on Santeria and Voodoo, and spirituality and magic.

In the corner of the shop by the entrance sits a small altar with a statue of the Virgin Mary, some crystals and blue stones. A small shell shaped bowl filled with grapes lays at the feet of the Virgin Mary. There is a white candle on top of the alter which Agnus lights every morning when she opens shop as she says a little prayer to Amaya.

Scattered throughout the shop are dozens of candles on display in all different colors, each one representing a different saint or Orisha as they are called in Agnus's Voodoo religion.

There is a small kitchen counter in the back of the room with a sink and an instant coffee pot on top, along with a shelf loaded with several different kinds of herbal teas in tin cannisters with colorful labels on them. All made by Agnus herself. The teas are made from dried flowers and herbs she cultivates in her tiny garden out back, and the labels are hand painted by Agnus as well.

Agnus has her back to Daisy as she walks over to the counter and takes a cannister of tea down from the shelf.

Daisy, dressed in a yellow and white sundress with her namesake printed all over it and a white ruffled collar, sits herself down in the middle of the settee and smooths the skirt of her dress out. She crosses her legs at the ankles, raises her chin, and strikes a pose like a little girl about to get her portrait painted. She frowns at the makeshift altar.

"Don't you give me no concoctions now, Agnus. I don't trust you. You're in cahoots with her, for all I know. For all I know, you're the one who brought her back to life."

"Child, what are you goin' on about?" Agnus straightens up and braces herself on the counter. She plugs the coffee pot in to make some hot water for the tea.

"It's her, I tell you, it's her. She's come back, and she went and bought the house."

"So, someone bought the house," Agnus says softly to herself.

"Well, what you gonna do?"

"Why, nothing, of course."

"Well, I'm not going to stand for it. She's not going to come back and upset my town again. I just won't have it." Daisy is visibly upset, shaking violently now.

"Child, calm yourself. Marina's been dead for twenty-five years now. It's not her. It's probably just someone that looks like her." Agnus pours hot water over a homemade teabag filled with herbs and spices, and hands Daisy the cup.

"Oh yeah? Looks just like her, and bought the house? I say that's too much of a coincidence for me. I'm getting ready, and you should too. I tell you, bad things are coming."

"How do you know she looks like her?" Agnus asks, but Daisy ignores the question because just then the door opens with a ring of the bells again, and in walks Lucy.

"Hello, Agnus. Hello, Daisy."

Daisy gets up from the settee.

"You better watch out—she's back and it's not good." She says as she brushes past Lucy with a huff and strides out the door, leaving the tea untouched and the two women looking after her in familiar bewilderment.

"What was that all about?" Lucy asks with a friendly smirk on her face.

"Oh, you know Daisy, she's crazy as a loon. Still living in the past. Somedays more than others. She's claiming Marina's back from the dead again. Here, have some tea. I just made this for Daisy, but she didn't touch it."

"Oh, no thank you, Agnus. I just stopped in to pick up some of those candles I love so much."

"She come running in here like a bat out of hell." Agnus chuckles as she walks over to the armoire where she displays her homemade candles in mason jars. She takes a vanilla-scented one off the shelf and proceeds to wrap it in tissue paper for Lucy.

"Poor thing," Lucy continues, "I think she peaked in high school, that's her problem. And Marina was her only foe. I think it makes her feel young again to have some competition, even if it's only in her imagination."

"Ah, well. We all want to feel young again. Can't say as I blame her for that." The old woman smiles.

Agnus has known Daisy and Lucy all their lives. They are getting on in years. They're in their twilight years, as they say. And Agnus, well, nobody knows just how old Agnus is, but she has memories as old as the town itself. Some say she's even older than the town, and she has the scars to prove it. And the wisdom.

"You know that guest cottage you have, Lucy?"

"Yes."

"I think you might want to put an ad in the paper for a renter."

"Why do you say that?"

"Just thinking out loud. Might be good for you, and might be good for somebody else, that's all." Agnus hands Lucy the little brown bag with the candle in it, all wrapped up in pink tissue paper, like a gift.

"How much do I owe you, Nissy?" Lucy reaches into her bag.

"Nothin' at all, child." Agnus smiles at the familiar nickname.

"Thank you, Nissy." Lucy reaches up and gives the tall old woman a peck on the cheek. "Actually, I think I might put my cottage up for rent. It's been awful lonely around the house lately. Be good to have some company again."

"That's a dear child. You come back soon now, you hear?" Agnus calls as Lucy strides out of the shop and into the sunny day.

Agnus lowers herself down onto the red velvet settee and takes the untouched cup of tea and sips the soothing hot liquid. She closes her eyes for just a minute and thinks back to the days when she was a young girl and working for Miss Cheralena.

Agnus was only nine years old back then, a stowaway from St. Croix and all alone in the world. But she was resourceful. She convinced Miss Cheralena to hire her and let her take care of her and her unborn baby. And take care of them she did.

She remembers the day Marina was born. Almost killed Miss Cheralena, she did, probably be better off if she had. Miss Cheralena was bleeding like there was no tomorrow. Agnus dressed her in white gauze and got her in the tub filled with milk and white carnations. She took white candles, fifty of them, and placed them all around her. Then she lit the candles and prayed to Obatala. She prayed all night while Miss Cheralena screamed and bled. Finally, Marina came out. Miss Cheralena passed out from either the pain or loss of blood, Agnus didn't know, but she was too busy to notice. She had to cut the cord and unwrap it from the poor little baby's neck. Being an island girl, Agnus sure saw her share of births, but she ain't seen nothin' like this before. She had to feed that baby sugar water for a full week before Miss Cheralena was well enough to nurse her proper.

She stayed with that family until the fateful day.

Poor baby girl. Agnus loved that child just like her own, but boy was she a handful. Agnus takes another sip of tea and thinks back to the days when Marina was a young girl, not yet a teenager. That's when the trouble started.

She's sitting in her mother's parlor contemplating death again. She seems to do this a lot lately. What does it actually mean, to die? Just to cease to exist. Just alive one moment and gone the next. She's not afraid of the process as much as the thought of being all alone. Nothingness is one thing but facing that all alone is something else.

There's a party going on in the ballroom again tonight. "Doesn't she realize that I have homework?" Marina thinks to herself. "Any minute she's going to be calling me to come out and join the party, I know it."

"Girl, where are you? Come on out here. Don't you know I need you to hostess the party?"

"Pleeease. Give me a break." Marina rolls her eyes.

"Go on out there and dance with the nice boys, will you?" her mother says sweetly. And then immediately hisses, "Do something to earn your keep around here. Go on up to room eight and bring these drinks to Mr. Smith. Hurry up now, girl."

"I wish I were dead," Marina thinks, "it must be better than this."

Mr. Smith is not much older than she, but he looks like he's seen better days. He is unshaven and stinks of alcohol and tobacco.

"Gross, I don't think he's brushed his teeth in a year," she thinks to herself.

She walks in and brings him the tray of drinks. He's alone in the room and he's drunk. He pulls Marina toward him and throws her on the bed, knocking the tray of drinks right out of her hand. "How disgusting." She struggles to get away from him and he falls on the floor. Marina runs out of the room. She's gonna get it for this tomorrow, she knows, but who cares.

"I hate her. I hate this. I hate living this way. I wish my father were alive." She starts to cry. The only solace in her day is school, but lately that too has become a nightmare. The kids at school are starting to call her names, like whore and bastard. They say her father wasn't her real father, and that she was born a bastard, illegitimate.

"Oh, Daddy. Where are you? Why did you have to die and leave me here in this hellhole?"

She runs to the kitchen, and falls into Agnus' arms, sobbing.

"Hide me, Nissy. Please hide me."

"There, there, child. It's ok now. You're safe with me," Agnus whispers as she takes Marina through the dining room and into the secret garden where no one will find them.

"Oh Nissy, what would I do without you? I hate it here so much; I want to die."

"Hush, child. Don't you ever say that. The wind god might hear you and take you away."

They're hiding in the secret garden and Agnus is stroking Marina's long black hair. "It's so nice out here tonight," Marina thinks. "Maybe the witch won't find me here."

"Marina! I said get on out there and mingle, will you?"

Marina releases herself from Agnus' hold and slips out the garden gate and runs all the way to the dock. She sits at the edge of the dock in the darkness. No one can see her here. She sits here to get away from the craziness. Not even her mother can find her here.

She looks into the water below. There is a sliver of a moon out tonight and it's throwing just enough light to show her reflection in the water. It makes her look older, and wiser somehow. Like another girl, but with the same face. Oh, how she wishes she were that other girl! She wishes she could get away. Run away. But where would she go? She doesn't know any place other than this backward town and she has no friends. Maybe that girl in the water will be my friend, she thinks. "Oh, please help me, girl in the water. Come and save me," she says to her reflection in the water.

"Marina! Marina, honey. Where are you, baby child?"

It's Agnus.

"Oh, Nissy. Oh, Nissy," she sobs, "why won't they leave me alone?"

Agnus comes up and wraps a shawl around Marina's shoulders.

"There, there, now, baby child. I told you, don't be out here on this pier alone at night. You're likely to fall in and drown, you hear? It's ok. You're ok now."

"Oh, Nissy, please don't make me go back in there, please."

"What's the matter, now baby child? Do tell your Nissy. Something happen at school today?"

"Only that bitch forgot my Halloween costume and I had to sit in the principal's office all day and watch the other kids have fun."

"Oh, honey, now you know she don't believe in no Halloween."

"I don't care what she's believes in. I hate her."

"Now, honey, don't go sayin' that, baby child."

"I do, I do, I hate her. I wish my father were alive and she was the one who was dead."

Agnus bows her head in anguish.

## SIX

"I hate to do it, but I know I have to get it over with right away before I chicken out."

It's Monday morning and we're boarding the plane back to New York, and I'm fretting about quitting my job. We land at LaGuardia at nine-thirty, and the plan is for me to go right in and tell them, but I've been fretting about this all weekend and don't know what to say.

"What are you going to tell them?" Michael asks.

"I don't know", I say.

"You can't tell them the truth. Then they'll know that I'm not far behind you, and that won't be good for either one of us."

"I know, I know. But I hate to lie."

"You'll have to think of something."

"I know, but what could I say that would sound believable anyway?"

"Why don't you tell them you have a medical condition and that you have to leave town to be treated?" he says.

"Are you kidding? They'll think I have cancer or something dreadful like that, and they'll pity me and give me those looks you see people get on their faces when they feel sorry for you, but are secretly relieved it's not them. Or worse yet, they'll think I'm an alcoholic and have to go into rehab!"

"They're not going to think that."

"What else would they think? And besides, it's bad luck to lie about being sick, it can bring it on, you know."

"Don't be ridiculous," Michael scoffs.

We argue back and forth like that for the entire flight, and in the end, decide to tell them Carly needs her mother, and I am going up to Boston for a while.

I know it sounds lame, but I can't think of anything else. Maybe they'll think Carly is pregnant or getting married or something happy like that. At least we won't be getting flowers and get-well cards delivered to the house.

I'm back at the office, sitting at my desk and looking out the window onto Seventh Avenue below. It's a crisp September day. One of the ten best days of the year according to the weather report. One of those days where the sky is so blue and there is not a cloud to be seen. Picture-perfect fall day in the city. Too bad it will be dark by five and freezing as soon as the sun sets. Then the rest of the winter will be grey and cloudy. I'm sick of the winters in New

York and feeling homesick for Villa Cheralena already, and I've only been back an hour.

"Hey, babe, have you told them yet?" Michael peeks his head in and catches me daydreaming.

"No. I'm planning on going in there right after lunch."

"Well, then, may I have the pleasure?" he asks as he bows at the waist and sweeps his arm forward like he's asking for a dance at the ball.

"Sure, just let me close my computer down. Where are we going?"

"I thought we might walk to the Plaza for lunch, it's such a nice day out. We could grab something downstairs at the cafeteria."

Ever since they redid the Plaza and added that food court in the basement, we've been going at least three times a week. We love it there. It feels like when we were in college and would go to the cafeteria for lunch. We even call it the cafeteria now. I turn off my computer and lock my door, and Michael and I set out for the elevator. We ride down the seventeen flights in less than two minutes and walk past the doorman and out into the sunshine. Then we turn toward the park and start walking.

"I can't wait to go back to Florida," I say, tucking my hand into his elbow like I've done every day since the day we started dating. Michael frowns as he bends his arm at the elbow to catch my hand.

"I've been thinking. I don't want you to go to the closing all by yourself. Let me see if I can fly down just for the day, at least. Then if something comes up, you won't have to deal with it all alone."

"Yeah, I guess you're right, that'll be nice," I say with a smile. I know he's going to miss me terribly. Can he even get along without me after all these years, I wonder?

"And, you never know, maybe we can…." he begins, with that hint of smile on his face that says he's thinking of something else, but he leaves it there because we've reached the entrance to the Plaza. We get separated in the crowd at the doors, and then meet back up again as we make our way into the hotel and head down the stairs to the food court. The food court at the Plaza has everything you could imagine. Coffee and French pastry, sushi, an Italian deli, a soup and salad place, an Irish pub, a hamburger joint.

"What shall it be?' Michael asks.

"How about soup and salad?" I say, as I always do.

"Soup and salad, it is," he says as he leads me to a table. It's nice because this place has table service, unlike some of the other ones where you have to walk up to the counter and order. I order the pumpkin squash soup and the arugula salad with goat cheese and beets, and Michael orders the Chinese chicken salad with peanut dressing, as usual. We are such creatures of habit. Is this comfortable habit a good thing or are we stuck in a rut?

I think back to the early years. We were so young, and so broke, and so much in love. I remember our first apartment. We were both so scared that we were over our heads with the rent that we couldn't look each other in the eyes that first morning for fear the other might see the truth there. It was a little two-room place in SoHo, back when SoHo wasn't so up and coming. It was a dump, really, but we wanted to be in the city so badly. It was a third-floor walk-up for $750 a month, and it hardly had any heat in the winter, no air conditioning in the summer, and we were lucky to get hot water in the morning. Our very own piece of paradise. We scrubbed and painted the walls. We sanded and refinished the wood floors ourselves (now we would get a flooring company to do that work). We scraped ten coats of paint off the window frames and sills and repainted them. We didn't care that we had to do all this work by ourselves, and we didn't dare ask the landlord to do it for us (he would have laughed us right out of the building). There was one big room with a brick wall on the back side, a kitchen to the right, and windows that looked right at the brick building next door. The bedroom had a fire escape, which we used as a balcony like everybody else did. SoHo balconies, we called them. God forbid there was ever a fire, we would all be dead with all the stuff we had on those fire escapes. Potted plants, hanging plants, and two beach chairs. You had to climb out the window, holding one beach chair up so you could sit in the one next to it, then the next person would just have to climb right into the chair. It wasn't easy, but we were young and thought it was fun. I loved that place. We ordered and built every stitch of furniture from Ikea (the bookshelves were a feat I'll never forget). They covered the entire back brick wall and held a stereo and all our design books. No TV back then. No time to watch it.

I knew back then that I would look back on those days as the good old days.

Now we're up to our eyeballs in condos that have to be completed so we can bill the clients before they pull the plug.

Michael is the Director of Design in the Architectural department, and I, the Director of Design in the Interior Design department of a large firm in New York. It's all about the billing there.

We were so green when we first started out in the design business, green from the inside out, working for the love of the work.

We both landed a job at the same firm, which was such a lucky break; I thought it was planned by some higher power. It has taken us ten years to move to the top of our fields, and now we no longer work for the love of the work. We work for billable hours. Yes, we are in the business of selling time, just like hookers.

Michael was asked to be a partner this year, but he's not going to take it. He doesn't want the stress or the liability. He doesn't want his name on the door because that means when they come to sue, it's his name on the papers as well. And condo work is extremely litigious. Not that they're making any real big mistakes, it's just that once the unit owners get in and form a Condo Board, they invariably start to look around to see who they can sue to recoup some money for the Association. It's a dirty game, but somebody has to play it. Lately we're in court more than on the job site, and that's no fun. It drains all our creative energy.

Life was fine while Carly was a little girl. I had something outside of work to pour my heart into. But now that Carly's gone, the life has gone out me, and I'm afraid, our marriage. We get up every morning and go to work, not strangers really, but almost living like brother and sister. No excitement anymore. Just doing the same thing day in and day out.

To open a bed and breakfast and work it as our "retirement" after Carly went away to college, that was always my dream. Well, Carly has been gone for a year now.

Carly, my sweet, sweet Carly. I remember standing on the train platform, suitcases in hand, holding on to her one last time. She practically had to pry my arms from around her to hop on that train.

And I remember the day she was born too, like it was yesterday. I was thirty-four years old and I never thought I'd have children. I always said I just wasn't the type. I didn't even like being around other people's kids, and I had no fond memories as a child myself. It just wasn't in the cards for me, that's what I thought, until one day something just clicked. The alarm on my biological clock started ringing, and suddenly I had an uncontrollable urge to be pregnant. I was so consumed with getting pregnant and being pregnant. And when I did finally get pregnant, it felt like my life had real meaning for the first time. I was fiercely protective of the process and my body, and my soon to be born child. And I was having the wildest dreams. Funny what hormones can do.

I remember our first fight—well, disagreement really. I was due any day and we were discussing baby names. I already knew it was a girl, and I had this dream the night before about a little girl. In the dream, the little girl introduced herself to me and said her name was Marina. It felt so real that I took it as a sign that it was my unborn child, and that we should name her Marina. I take my dreams seriously. I always believed that my dreams were my intuition speaking to me, especially when I was pregnant. But Michael just laughed and said there was no way he would name his baby girl after a boat dock. He had an aunt who died when he was very young, and her name was Carly. He loved that aunt so much, so in the end, who could argue with that?

But now I really don't mind at all. She's perfect no matter what we call her. Carly is beautiful and smart and talented, and on her way to becoming a successful fashion designer.

And soon it is going to be my turn to live again, finally.

I sip my soup and we eat our salads and people watch in silence until it's time to go back to work.

As we walk hand in hand back to the office, I notice my reflection in the shop windows. I'm still in pretty good shape for a fifty-three-year-old woman. And Michael is still so handsome with his full head of black hair. We are both healthy and we have a beautiful, healthy daughter. We have interesting and successful careers, a great social life, and a happy marriage. One couldn't ask for more. Then why am I not satisfied with my life? I know I should be so very grateful for all that I have, but there is a void deep down inside of me. And wrapped around that void, a feeling of discontent, and it's been slowly creeping up, trying to surface.

That night we order take out from the market down the street. As we eat lasagna from the cocktail table in front of the TV, I look around at the apartment I fell in love with just one year ago. We were lucky to get this apartment for the price: $10,000 a month all included. And two parking spaces on the street. 1500 square feet of paradise in the city. In the summertime, I grow herbs on the rooftop garden, and we grill outside and entertain friends. From there you can see the West Side Highway and the Hudson River beyond. It's perfect New York City living. We walk to the market and the bookstore and take the subway to work when we're not working too late.

A two-bedroom, two-bath row house on the Upper West Side. The front door is ten stairs up, and the living room, kitchen, and dining room are on that level. The master bedroom suite is on the third level, and there is a tiny little garden on the roof. There is another bedroom and bath on the ground level, which Michael and I share as an office. There are window boxes in the windows in which I plant tulips in the spring, and geraniums in the summer. Right now, there is boxwood growing, the only thing that will stay alive in the winter months. Come Christmas I'll decorate them with tiny little white lights and hang a wreath on the door.

The living room is decorated in the neoclassical style, with a carved mahogany cocktail table and end tables to match. There's an overstuffed camel-colored crushed velour sofa in front of the fireplace, and a wool Persian rug on the hardwood floor. There are caramel-colored velvet drapes on the windows with swags and tie-backs, and tan shades underneath that let in the light during the day and keep the privacy at night. The TV hangs over the fireplace, the only place it would fit, since Michael insisted on a sixty-inch flat screen. A true decorator's house apart from that one detail.

After dinner, we take the fur throw and all the pillows off the sofa and lay them on the rug. We sit in front of the fire, sipping brandy.

"What's the matter, honey? You've been awful quiet tonight", Michael says.

"Oh nothing, just a little melancholy, I guess."

"Are you sure you want to do this project?"

"It's a little late for that kind of question, don't you think? I just quit my job today."

"You can always come back if you want, you know that", he says.

"I don't know what I want."

"Well, I know what I want."

Michael takes the brandy from my hand and places it on the coffee table behind us. He slips his hand under my blouse and gently caresses my back as he plants baby kisses on my neck.

This used to thrill me, but tonight I just go along, detached but cooperative. We make love on the floor in front of the fire. Ten years ago, this would be the most romantic thing I could think of. Tonight, I'm just not feeling much of anything.

It's quiet now, and all I can hear are the sounds of Michael breathing and the radiator humming. I smell the scent of the goldenrod sitting on the end table in the blue Ming vase that my mother gave us for a wedding present.

Michael stirs and stretches. "What time is it?"

"It's exactly 12:00," I say. "You looked so peaceful sleeping there I didn't want to wake you."

"Thanks. And thanks for dinner, my love," he says as he pinches me in the side lightly. "Are you sure you're gonna be able to cook for all our guests at our new hotel? Do you even remember how to cook?"

"Yes, I do," I say, pretending to be upset. "And besides, it's not a hotel, it's a bed and breakfast." I punch him gently in the stomach and he plays along and pretends to buckle over with the blow.

"Well, I get the bed part, but what about breakfast?" he jokes as he heads toward the bedroom.

I pick up the blanket and the pillows and throw them back on the sofa.

Michael walks over and rearranges them. Always neat, always perfect, all the time.

I lay in bed trying to fall asleep, and when sleep comes, it's restless and fitful.

*I'm walking through a house. It's a house that I know by heart. I walk past the foyer, and into the dining room. There is a fireplace in the dining room. I crawl up through the fireplace and into a secret room. There are no windows in this room, there is only room to sit cross-legged with my head bowed. This is my secret hiding place, where no one can find me. I'm eight years old and*

*I am hiding, but I feel safe here and I'm not afraid. I just want to sit here and hide and listen to the grownups talking in the dining room on the other side. I love this house because it has a lot of rooms, and a lot of different hiding places. Now I crawl over to another space and I'm in a different room, behind the wall, listening to the people on the other side. There is music playing and the smell of cigars and whiskey is in the air. The grownups are drinking and laughing. I want to be part of that party, but I know I don't belong. I don't belong to these people at all. I'm happy just to sit here in my little hiding spot inside the walls. And now I can't get out from inside the walls, but I'm still not afraid. I just want to stay here where I feel safe. I curl up and fall asleep.*

I wake up suddenly. I've had this dream many times before. I lie in bed and try to conjure up the house, but I can't. All I can remember is the familiar feeling I had being there. Slowly, the dream fades away, as dreams always do.

## SEVEN

It's Halloween. We closed on the old house yesterday. I'm dressed all in white and I'm sitting on the porch of my soon-to-be-new bed and breakfast. I have a bucket of candy at my side. I've attached my new business cards to each piece, with a hole punch and a little piece of orange ribbon. The card reads:

*Villa Cheralena*
*Under new Ownership*
*Opening November, 2012*

That's exactly one year from tomorrow. I hope we make it. We've already done the drawings and hired the contractor. The demolition starts Monday morning. It should be a six-month job, but I know how these things can be. Usually, any job is at least three months late, and the renovations are sometimes more. You never know what you're going to find once you knock down a wall or tear out a cabinet. There could be rot, or worse yet, black mold hiding behind those walls. Then we would be forced to tear the whole thing down to the studs, replace them, and rehang all new drywall. That's a very big and expensive job and would set us back a few months at least.

But this house has good bones, I can feel it. And there are no signs of water intrusion that I can see. As long as it's dry, it's not rotted or moldy.

Michael flew home yesterday right after the closing and left me here to get things organized before the big day. He plans on coming back next Saturday and I miss him already. But it's a beautiful night. The full moon is just rising now over the water, and I have a bottle of wine by my side and a bucket full of candy to give out. Hopefully, I will get a chance to meet some neighbors walking with their children, knocking on doors for Halloween. So far, it's six o'clock and I haven't seen anyone come by, but it's not yet dark out, so I sit back and take a sip of my merlot and enjoy the warm breeze.

I've taken orange paper bags and cut out jack-o'-lantern faces in them and filled them with some sand and a candle. The walk from the street all the way to the top of the terrace steps is bordered on both sides with my homemade jack-o'-lanterns. It looks welcoming and not scary. I didn't want to decorate the house in a scary way. I don't believe Halloween should be about that anyway. Halloween is for kids. Why should we try to scare them?

I see a group of goblins, ghosts, pirates, and princesses walking down the street, right past my jack-o'-lanterns and my house.

"Hello!" I say and wave. Trying to get them to see that I am sitting here waiting to give them treats.

One of the pirates screams and runs away, and the rest follow. Now the moms are walking by.

"Hello!" I say again. "I didn't mean to scare anybody," I say, sounding ridiculous. It's Halloween after all.

The moms hurry by and head up the next street, looking the other way, pretending not to notice me at all.

"What is going on here?" I say to myself.

I see another group, this time they are older kids, and they are laughing and shouting at me.

"Hey, lady, are you the ghost?" one of the boys says, and they all run away.

It's dark out by now, probably around seven, and the streets are filled with trick-or-treaters, but no one has come up the walk to my house. I decide to turn on all the lights inside the house to show them that there is someone living here now. Maybe they just don't know who I am and are afraid to come? I go inside and switch on all the lights, which aren't that many because there is no furniture in the house, just the hallway fixtures and the chandeliers and such. As I come back outside, I see a lady walking up to my door.

"Hello," I say, "I'm Teresa."

"I know who you are", she says.

She is probably about sixty years old, but in her Halloween costume she looks like she's sixteen. She's dressed in a pleated plaid skirt and knee socks with saddle shoes and she's carrying a large bible. Her long blonde hair, probably extensions, is tied in low pig tails. I can tell even in this light that she was once a beauty, high cheek bones, big eyes. Looks like she was once stunning but has had too many face jobs of late. She is wearing a ridiculously large pin on the collar of her white button-down shirt. I invite her to sit on one of the rockers and pour myself another glass of wine.

"Glass of wine?" I ask, as I pour another glass of merlot and offer it to her.

"You shouldn't be drinking that", she says, and she looks around to see if anybody's looking, before she sits down, straight backed, in the rocking chair next to me.

"I just bought this house yesterday," I say. "My husband and I plan on renovating it and turning it into a bed and breakfast."

"Why? Why would you want to do that?" she says.

I don't understand the question, but I let it go.

"Tell me something. Why aren't the trick-or-treaters coming for candy?" I ask, deciding to get right to the point with this woman. I can sense she came here to tell me something, anyway, might as well get right to it.

"Halloween is a pagan holiday. You shouldn't be here, your momma's gonna whip you. Why did you come back?"

"Come back?" I ask.

"You know, I'm an actress now and I'm famous." She stands up and gives a little curtsey as if to prove it. "That's right. I could have been really famous, like Sharon Stone. I could have had her part in that movie, but I didn't want to sleep with the director, so they gave it to her instead.".

Dumbfounded, I just nod. I realize just how ridiculous she looks in her schoolgirl costume.

"But that's ok, because I'm a famous actress anyway", She continues. "I work at the Historical Society you know, and I give the trolley tours. Everybody knows me."

She gets up and bends over me, one hand on the arm of my rocker, and looks into my eyes intently. "Where were you all these years anyway?"

I don't know what to say, so I just sit there, eyes wide. A large crucifix falls out from her buttoned-down shirt and is dangling in my face, so close it almost hits me in the nose.

"You know, they tried to tear your house down, but I wouldn't let them. I work for the Historical Society after all. They wanted to tear it down, but I wouldn't let them. I told them to condemn the pier though, and you should thank me for that you know."

"Who's they?" I ask. What the hell is this crazy woman talking about?

She's fidgeting like a teenager, unable to stand still, and then suddenly her whole expression changes and she straightens up and says; "The Christ is coming. The final judgement day is near. Only the blood of Christ can save you now."

She must be role playing, I think, to prove she was an actress. It's almost comical, if it wasn't so frightening. Maybe she's a lunatic. Maybe I should call for help.

"This house has been a place of sin for a long time. They wanted to burn it down after the old lady died, but I wouldn't let them."

"Who's they?" I ask again.

"Why, everybody, my dear. All your neighbors. Not me, of course. I'm on the historical board after all. I love old houses," she says with a tight smile.

She can't be serious, can she?

"Why did you come back?" She demands.

"Excuse me?" I ask. She's really starting to frighten me.

Then she starts again; "Save yourself. Commit yourself to the blood of Christ before it's too late or burn in Hell! The time has come, the day is upon us, the end of days is near. Halleluiah, praise God, the final judgement day is near!

Then she bends down over me again and looks right into my eyes, as if searching for some unknown clue.

"I knew this house was haunted, and now you're here......"

"I have no idea what you're talking about," I say defensively. She seems to be going in and out of different personalities and I'm wondering how I'm going to get away from her before she becomes violent.

Then she abruptly changes the subject again, as if she were another person noticing my unease. Her entire facial expression changes, so much so that she looks like a different person.

"My name is Daisy. I live just down the street in the orange house with the fountain in the front. You're welcome anytime for coffee or just to chat if you get to feeling lonely. The townspeople can be kind of cruel, you know. I hold a bible study every Wednesday morning, please do come by."

"Thank you, I will", I lie.

She seems normal now. She must have been in character. Just some crazy actress dressed up for Halloween.

"Well, good luck", she says and skips down the walk, clutching her bible, like a little girl. on her way to school.

That woman's crazy. And to think, she actually believes the house is haunted, and on Halloween no less. What is this, the eighteenth century? Oh well, maybe the ghost stories will be a good marketing tool. People love to stay in haunted mansions. Maybe I'll even call those ghost hunters on the History Channel and see if they want to do a special. Maybe they can even do a side story on Daisy, the ex-movie star.

I get up to pour some more wine and notice the bottle is empty. Did I drink that whole bottle? No matter, I'm feeling a little woozy anyway. I don't think I should have any more. I look at my watch and it is eleven. Wow, where did the time go? And I have all this candy! Guess I'll bring it to the homeless shelter or the hospital or something tomorrow. And I made all those business cards and didn't even get to hand out one of them. I'm feeling a little depressed and very tired all of a sudden, and my head is pounding.

I walk back into the house.

Maybe I'll just lie down for a little bit in the back room. The maid's room is the only room that is still furnished. I walk down the small hallway leading from the kitchen to the small bedroom. The single bed is made up with clean white sheets and a yellow cotton throw. I wonder why they didn't take this furniture out of here? Was this bed made up when we first looked at the house? I can't remember. Maybe our realtor is using this room to cheat on his wife or something. I've heard of stranger things before, especially in Palm Beach. Let me just lie down here for a little bit before I try to drive back to the hotel in my condition. No use getting pulled over on Halloween for drunken driving. That won't be too good for my reputation in this town. I laugh to myself at the image of my mugshot in the morning's paper, as I lay my head down on the pillow. Somewhere in the distance, as I drift off to sleep, I hear a door slam shut.

*I'm twelve years old and I'm in school. It's Halloween and all the other kids are dressed up in their costumes, but not me. My mother is so out of it, she forgot to buy me a costume. I'm devastated. The only one to go to school without a Halloween costume. I have to sit in the principal's office and watch all the other kids in the entire school parade around the grounds as pirates and fairies and princesses. There'll be a contest at the end of the day to see who has the best costume and they'll award the winners with candy. My teacher found me earlier, crying in the back room. Having come to school unprepared, I was utterly humiliated when I realized I not only had no costume, but that I once again was singled out as the outcast. Not included in the schoolyard games, left out, different than the rest.*

*Anger, resentment, and shame start to boil inside of me. I see a big black witch's pot on the fire. Anger, resentment, and shame start to boil in the brew. I can hear the other children laughing at me and calling me names like bastard and whore. I stir the pot with a long wooden spoon. Anger, resentment, and shame. I can see the flames now, burning orange and red like the sunset over the trees. I can see the black smoke coming out of the pot now. Anger, resentment, and shame. Now I can smell the smoke and I can hear the crackling of the fire.*

*FIRE!*

*She stands across the street and watches as the flames leap out of the back window.*

I wake up to smoke all around me. There are flames shooting out from the hallway leading to the kitchen. Fire! Oh, my God, I fell asleep and the house caught on fire. The house is on fire. That is all that my mind can register in my shock and panic. Finally,

I grope around for my phone and dial 911, but I realize someone must have already called because before I can speak, I hear the fire engines pull up. Then it occurs to me that I'd better tell them I'm in the house. I didn't tell anybody I was going to sleep here last night, in fact I didn't even know myself, and then I realized I had too much wine and I didn't want to drive back to the hotel at—

"Operator, what is your emergency?"

"Help! I'm in the house!" My mind is racing, trying to go over everything that happened last night.

"What house is that, ma'am?"

"The house! The house that's burning! The house that's on fire! The fire trucks are here, and I don't think they know I'm in here. Nobody knows I'm in here!" Help me, please." I remember hearing a door slam right before I fell asleep. Or was it the sound of something else? A small explosion perhaps? Like a pop or a crack.

"Please calm down, ma'am, and tell me where you are."

Suddenly I realize I'm talking like a crazy person, and I try to calm down. I'm on the floor now with the yellow blanket over my head, trying to keep the smoke out of my lungs, like they taught me to do in grade school.

"The address is 200 Granada Road, West Palm Beach. The house is on fire and the firemen don't know that I am trapped inside in the back bedroom by the kitchen," I say as calmly as I can. I can feel the heat on the floor now, I can feel the heat in my lungs, and I am coughing and crawling towards the back window.

"Try to stay calm now, somebody is coming to get you out of there," the dispatcher says.

Suddenly someone breaks the window and glass falls all over me.

"Is anybody in here?"

"Here I am," I say, feeling a wave of relief wash over me like thick warm water, or is that my blood?

The fireman climbs through the window and picks me up in one swoop and lifts me out of the window and into another's arms waiting just outside. He carries me to the firetruck. I'm coughing and bleeding from a piece of glass that flew into my upper left arm when he broke the window, but I'm alive.

They wrap me in a blanket and put an oxygen mask on my face and leave me sitting there on the curb and go back to contain the fire. I sit and watch the back portion of the house that is the hallway between the kitchen and the room I was sleeping in. There are flames shooting up and out in all directions. There is smoke everywhere, so much smoke. The firemen are aiming their hoses directly into the broken window that I was just pulled out of.

Finally, the flames subside, the smoke puffs out in one last spiteful cloud, and in what seems like hours but is probably just a few minutes, the fire is out.

What the hell just happened? I start to cry. I remember the dream I was having. Am I crying for me or am I crying for that little girl in my dream? I think I might have just died; I think I'm just crying in relief. I need to get out of here and lie down. I can feel the all too familiar migraine starting to work its way from my stomach up into my temples. Pounding like an ancient Indian war drum.

Just then the paramedics pull up and they take me into the van. I'm sitting in the back of the van with the doors open. They are taking my vitals and asking me questions about what had happened—who am I, and how do I feel? And I'm crying like a baby.

"Must be in shock," I hear someone whisper.

"No, no. I'm fine, I'm fine." I say to no one in particular.

I see a crowd starting to form outside the van. All my new neighbors are standing there in a little circle, watching me and whispering to each other, but no one walks up to me or offers me any words of kindness. Just then I see a young girl in a long white skirt standing off to the side, away from the crowd. I can see her clearly in the moonlight. She has no shoes on. She looks familiar and she has a puzzled look on her face, as if she recognizes me as well. Just then she disappears into the shadows as the paramedic tries to coax me into lying down.

"Ok, then, just rest here for a bit while I tend to your wound."

The paramedic is a young woman with blonde hair and kind eyes. She cleans and dresses the cut on my arm from the flying glass, lays me back on the stretcher, and puts a pillow under my head and a blanket over me.

I close my eyes.

I know the police are standing right outside the vehicle waiting to ask me questions, but I'm not ready yet to answer them. I just need a minute to gather my control and my courage.

It takes all night to clean up the scene. The sun is rising now, over the water like a giant red beach ball. I sit up and sip the coffee that someone has so kindly handed me, and give my statement to the police.

"Just tell us what happened, ma'am."

"I don't know what happened. I just fell asleep and the next thing I knew the house was on fire."

"Did you hear anything strange or see anything strange before you fell asleep?" one of the detectives asks.

"No." Did I hear a sound?

"What were you doing sleeping in this empty house all alone? Were you all alone?" The other one asks.

"Of course, I was all alone." Is it against the law to sleep in your own house? I think of asking, but I don't want to prolong the interview in any way.

"I told you, I was feeling dizzy, so I went to lie down for a while before I went back to my hotel for the night."

"Well, if you think of anything more, give one of us a call," the nice detective says, and hands me his card. Jeremy Williams, Lieutenant Sergeant. I'm certainly not going to call that other jerk.

"There was one thing. That girl. That girl in the white dress. Maybe she knows something." I say, almost to myself.

"What girl?"

"There was a girl standing there, right over there, looking at me. I get the feeling she knows something."

"Where did she go?"

"I don't know. She just disappeared," I say.

"Have you been drinking?" asks the jerk, holding the empty bottle of merlot and the two wine glasses he obviously just found in the kitchen during his inspection.

*Brilliant job, Sherlock*, is what I think to say, but instead say, "Yes, I shared a bottle of wine with a friend."

"And what friend was that, Mrs. Peters? I thought you said you were alone?"

"I don't know, I mean, it was a neighbor. She said her name was Daisy, she said she lived in the orange house down the street." I sound suspicious even to myself now and am worried that they might think I'm lying.

They look at each other over my head, and I know right away I said the wrong thing, but I don't know why. The mean detective steps away a few feet and pulls Sgt. Williams closer and whispers something to him.

"Let me take you back to your hotel, Mrs. Peters," Sgt. Williams says as he leads me to the squad car.

"What is it? What did he say to you?" I ask when we get into the car.

"Oh, nothing. You're going to be fine. What you need is a good night sleep and you'll be fine. But I know he's lying. It has something to do with Daisy. They both know Daisy; I can tell by the way they looked at each other when I said her name. Would she really try to burn my house down? Is she that crazy?

We're driving over the bridge now, and the sun is already high in the sky. It's going to be another scorcher. I don't think I'll sleep any more today. I feel the migraine pounding in my temples. That drum is calling the tribe to war.

## EIGHT

It's two in the afternoon, and I'm back at the Breakers, still lying in bed. Michael was notified about the fire and is on his way back down. His flight lands at two-thirty. I offered to pick him up at the airport, forgetting that I left the rental car at the house last night, but he told me to stay put. He's treating me like a child again. I know he got scared when he heard about last night, but that's no reason to treat me like a child. It's not as if I started the fire myself.

Sgt. Williams said the fire was probably caused by a faulty electrical wire and that it was very common in those old houses. I told Michael so when he called. Sgt. Williams also said I was lucky I woke up when I did, and I was lucky that someone called 911 when they did, or I would be dead, and the entire house would be burned down. That, I did not tell Michael.

I wonder, who did call 911?

I try not to think about it while I wait for my husband to arrive. But I can't stop thinking about that girl in white. Who is she? What was she doing there? And where did she go? She looked so familiar. And what about that dream I was having? It feels like I somehow started the fire in my dream, but I know that's impossible.

I've got to pull myself together. I'm more determined now than ever to prove to Michael that I can handle this job. I'm afraid he's going to call the whole thing off and put the house back up on the market and I do not want that to happen. For some reason I can't explain, I feel a strong connection to that old house now, and I do not want to sell. Not now, not ever.

This is going to be my new life and my new business. I am going to make this happen no matter what. I need this. No fire or rain or wind, or anybody, living or dead, is going to stop me.

"Honey?"

Michael opens the door to the suite and walks over to the bed. He gives me a gentle, awkward hug and sits down on the edge of the bed next to me.

"Are you ok?"

"I'm fine." I say, a little short-tempered. I don't mean to be short with him, but I hate when he walks on eggshells around me. I get up with the intention of getting dressed and force a smile. Just then my head starts pounding and I feel dizzy and fall back onto the bed.

"Oh my god. You're not fine. I'm calling the doctor." Michael has a look of panic on his face.

"No, no, I'm fine," I say. This time my smile is genuine. In fact, I almost giggle because of the look on his face.

"I guess I just need to sleep for a while."

"You lay down and take a nap. I'll be right here when you wake up," he says in that fatherly way of his.

"Ok, just a few minutes," I say as I drift off to sleep.

Michael reaches into his carry-on bag and pulls out his laptop. He flips it open and puts it on his lap, as he sits in the chair by the bed. He props his feet up on the edge of the bed and proceeds to open his e-mail account. "Might as well get some work done," he thinks, as he scrolls down the thirty or so e-mails he's received since leaving the city this morning. He saves the less pressing ones for later and opens the one marked 'urgent' first. The contractor on West 48th needs some R.F.I.'s answered or he's threatening to hold up the job. "I really didn't need this distraction today," Michael thinks. Now that he knows Teresa's ok, he regrets wasting another whole day coming down here. "I was going to be here next week-end anyway. Couldn't she have waited until then to get herself into trouble? We've owned the place for exactly one day and she's burning it down already."

He answers the R.F.I.'s off the top of his head and forwards them to his draftsman Todd with detailed instructions for him to send verification and back-up drawings to the contractor. Todd could handle these by himself Michael knows, but he just can't afford to risk him making a mistake or omitting something. He reminds Todd to copy him on the reply and moves on. Next, the e-mails from other clients: "When are we meeting next? Where are in the process? When can we submit the drawings for permit? He answers each one with calm and precise explanations, although inside he's anything but calm. "I really thought I'd have this day to catch up after missing a whole day of work on Thursday to come down here for the closing, and now this", he thinks.

Michael opens the last e-mail. It's from Sheila, the Bookkeeper. She says the usual gang is going to Sardi's tonight for drinks and some laughs, and since he's all alone in the city, she wonders would he like to join them? "But unfortunately, I'm not all alone in the city," he thinks. "I'm down here in Florida, babysitting my wife who can't seem to take care of herself."

"Thanks, but no thanks," he replies. He knows he would have had a good time at Sardi's with the usual gang, which lately consists of Sheila and a couple of other girls from accounting. They're all young and pretty and they never talk about work or renovating old houses for that matter. Sheila has a witty, dry sense of humor and she's intelligent, and Michael enjoys her company. Not that he's dating her or anything, he's a married man and doesn't cheat on his wife. Just a few drinks with the girls from accounting, that's all. He's been out with them a couple of times before, no big deal. But if he ever were going to cheat on his wife, it would probably be with Sheila. She's got a set on her and she's certainly willing.

Michael sees Teresa thrashing around in the bed, obviously having a bad dream. He snaps his laptop shut and places it on the nightstand. He gently shakes Teresa's shoulders and she calms down. "Probably out for the night", he thinks, so he quietly gets up and leaves her sleeping, then he heads downstairs for a drink at the bar.

# NINE

*It's a warm, sunny day and she's at the beach. School is finally out for the summer. She's sitting on her towel in her usual spot, with her toes in the sand, reading a book. Some kids from school are over there by the other side of the wall playing in the water. There is a stretch of beach behind one of the mansions where all the kids go. The house sits atop a hill and there is a ten-foot seawall at the shoreline. It's a private beach, but the kids hang out in front of that wall so the owners can't see them. The other kids are calling her names and making fun of her, so she gets up and goes into the water to get away from them. The water is unusually rough today and there is no lifeguard where they are. The tide is coming in fast. She doesn't want to hear those things they are saying to her, it makes her feel ashamed and angry. She's standing in the rough surf now, and suddenly the waves are breaking way over her head. She has to jump to keep on top of them. She tries to get out, but the tide has come in and she is trapped between the ocean and the seawall. The other kids are pointing and laughing at her. They are calling her whore and bastard. She's crying now and struggling to get out of the water. The waves are getting higher and higher, crashing into the seawall behind her with such force that she's afraid she will be smashed up against it. She can no longer jump over them and she's getting tired. She goes under in a panic, her arms flailing wildly. The waves are getting more forceful now and she is being smashed up against the wall over and over again.*

*She goes under again, tumbling and thrashing in the white foam, trying desperately to keep her head above the water, gasping for air.*

*"Help!"*

"Help—I'm drowning!"

"Honey. Wake up. Are you ok?" Michael has me by the shoulders and is gently shaking me.

"What? – Where?" I'm confused and disoriented.

"You were dreaming," he says. "My God, you're soaking wet."

It's dark outside and the only light on in the room is coming from the bathroom. He lets go of me and I get up and go into the bathroom without a word and turn on the shower. Maybe I have the flu or something. My body is aching all over and I'm freezing cold, and my clothes are soaking wet. I feel like death itself.

I slip off my wet clothes and get into the hot shower. Has he been sitting there in the dark watching me the whole time while I was sleeping? I need to get him out of here. I need to convince him that I'm ok, so he'll go back to New York tomorrow. I let the hot water run down my back and try to pull myself together. What a nightmare. I step out of the shower, wrap myself in a bathrobe and walk back into the bedroom. I notice Michael has stripped down to his underwear and t-shirt and is sitting up in the bed. I switch on the lamp at the bedside table.

"Sorry, honey. I didn't mean to scare you. I'm ok, really, I am. I was just overtired, and I guess I had a nightmare, but I'm just fine now," I lie. "Let's go to dinner. Did you make reservations somewhere?"

"No. I didn't make reservations somewhere," he says, sarcastically.

What the hell's the matter with him now?

"It's four in the morning!" He sounds mad.

"Did you eat?"

No reply. He is mad.

"I told you I was fine. You didn't have to stay in the dark and watch me sleep all night." I'm starting to feel defensive.

He's probably mad because he didn't get to eat dinner. I hope he got some sleep or he's going to be impossible to deal with in the morning. Poor baby didn't get to go to dinner in that fancy suit that he came down here in. I told him I was ok. He didn't have to stay and watch me sleep. I get back in bed and he turns off the light and rolls over on his side, facing away from me. I lie on my back, wide awake, looking up at the ceiling fan slowly marking the time. It's an eternity before I hear his heavy breathing slow down and get quiet; he's finally asleep.

I slip out of bed and go back to the bathroom, grabbing a T-shirt and shorts on my way. I quietly get dressed and slip out of the room. There's a little cafe down by the gift shops, but it's closed at this hour, so I head down to the beach.

The early morning clouds are pink and orange, and the sun's rays are fanned out over the sky like a child's drawing in a coloring book. The sun itself, an orange ball of fire is rising now from under the sea, breaking the darkness and changing the colors of the sea and sky. A flock of seagulls fly south, low to the water, hunting for breakfast in the bounty just below the surface.

The ocean is as calm as glass and there is not a soul in sight. I walk north along the water's edge, taking my time, looking at the shells and sea glass exposed by the outgoing tide. The air is slightly cool, and the water is warm and smells of salt. The sun is rising fast now in the southern sky, and it warms my shoulders as I bend over to examine a shell in the surf. There is a quiet, soothing rhythm to this morning sea, and I can almost hear it say, "Shush now, shush now, everything's going to be ok." There is something spiritual about the space between the sea and the sand during a sunrise.

I start to relax. I feel a little better now, the sea and the air are working their magic on me. I lift my head and look ahead in the direction I'm walking when suddenly I notice it, off in the distance. It's a wall, a seawall. Oh, my God, can it be? I'm looking at the wall from my nightmare and it's exactly as I dreamt it. I rack my brain, trying to remember if I had ever walked this far down the beach before, and if I had ever actually seen this wall in real life before, but I don't think so. I walk up and touch it just to make sure it is real. There is a water line near the bottom of the wall where it sits in the sand, and sure enough, it looks like the high tide does come right up to it. In fact, the water line is about a foot up the wall. It must be low tide, because I see a concrete ledge sticking out of the sand at the bottom. It looks like a good place to sit and read a book when it's low tide, and no, the owners of the property wouldn't be able to see if someone were sitting here from inside the house, which is quite a distance away from the wall itself and up on a gradual slope of lawn.

I have had dreams from time to time in my life about mundane events that came true. I used to think it was kind of special—neat, really. But now I'm feeling uneasy, and frankly, spooked by it. I don't like this one bit. I wonder if I should tell someone about it. Should I tell Michael? Shit, Michael! His plane leaves in a couple of hours. I hurry back down the beach toward the hotel. I have to get back to the room before he wakes up and starts to worry. Oh, my God, he'll never leave if he thinks I'm not ok in any way. I realize I can't possibly tell him about my dream and the seawall now; I'll never get rid of him.

The sun is high in the sky by now and the colors in the clouds are all gone. It's going to be another hot one today. I walk quickly back to the hotel, breaking a sweat. Not sure if it's my nerves or the sun.

All I can think about is making sure Michael gets on that plane. I open the door to the suite as quietly as is possible. But with a hotel key card and latch, that is nearly impossible, which is to say I make a racket. But no matter, Michael is already up and dressed.

"Where were you?" He looks upset. Shit, I should have brought him coffee.

"I went for a walk on the beach," I say, trying to sound casual.

He looks at my sandy feet and this seems to satisfy him. What, does he think I'm cheating on him? Where else would I be at this time of day?

"Let's go down for breakfast, my plane leaves in a few hours," he says curtly.

I'm already in the bathroom with my feet in the tub, rinsing off the sand. "Ok, I'll be right out," I say, trying to sound cheerful, but I can feel the tension in the air.

We walk down to the dining room in total silence. The hostess greets us with a warm smile and sits us by the picture windows facing the beach. Michael orders bacon and eggs and coffee, and I, an English muffin and coffee. An old Fleetwood Mac song is playing softly in the background as the waitress brings the food.

"Rock on gold dust woman

Follow those who pale in your shadow

Rulers make bad lovers

You'd better put your kingdom up for sale"

We sit in silence and eat our breakfast. Michael looks down at his plate, and I look out to sea. I feel like we are literally drifting apart. I'm on the crest of one wave heading out to sea, and Michael is in the valley of another. We can't even see each other anymore; the wave that's taking me out to sea is a wall between us.

Stevie Nicks continues to sing:

"Well did she make you cry

Make you break down

Shatter your illusions of love?

And is it over now

Do you know how

To pick up the pieces and go home?"

"Check, please!" Michael calls out, as if Stevie herself just gave him the ok. "There's no sense in you coming with me to the airport, since we have two cars. I'll just drop you off at the house, so you can get your car and then I'll go on to the airport."

This might be the first time that I have not driven him to the airport to say goodbye. He looks worried and sick, but I'm not sure I care. I just can't wait to get rid of him.

"Ok, that's fine with me." I shrug.

Michael goes upstairs to get his things, as I hand his parking ticket to the valet and wait for him in the lobby.

We drive to the house in silence.

"I guess this is goodbye, then." I say, forcing a little smile as I open the passenger door to get out.

"Take care of yourself, Teresa." He never calls me by my first name. "And try to be careful."

I sense he thinks the trip back down here was a big waste of time for him. He leans over and kisses me quickly on the lips. It feels so final.

I'm standing in the overgrown parking lot at Villa Cheralena and waving goodbye as Michael's car slowly rolls down the tree-lined street and finally disappears around the corner. I walk over to the pool and sit down on one of the stone benches by the garden wall and start to cry. I suddenly feel all alone. It's funny, just a moment ago I couldn't wait to get rid of him and now all I see ahead is this great big empty grey abyss. How will I fill the days without him? I remember when Carly first went off to college. I was a mess. I didn't know what to do with my days. One day I had this life, this role as mother with all the things that go along with that, and then I was standing on the train platform waving goodbye, and then it was over. Carly was gone, and I was left with nothing. No more early morning kisses. No more gossip about her friends at school. No more long mother-daughter talks at night. I remember thinking that I had to reinvent myself. Find another foundation to base my self-worth on. Oh, I had my work and Michael, but it wasn't the same. Carly was my whole life for eighteen years. She was my total focus. Eventually, I came out of it. My focus shifted back to Michael and our new lives as empty nesters. I forced him to take me to museums and concerts on the weekends, and out to dinner and dancing in the evenings. Finally, that scaled down to a normal pace as we got back into the groove of being alone with each other again. But this time, this time feels different. I don't want to lose him, but on the other hand, I have this feeling that I need to find myself again, and the only way to do that is to be alone for a while. But I'm scared, really scared for the first time in a long time. Scared to be alone. Scared of what I might find. The late morning sunlight is playing with the shadows of the leaves on the trees overhead. The garden is alive with sounds and movement and light, all familiar and yet somehow strange. I feel a hand on my shoulder and jump up, but there's no one there.

I've got to pull myself together. I've been in worse situations than this before. I just need to pretend the last few days never happened. Just push it out of my mind and move on. I'm good at that. I know how to compartmentalize, that's how I've always survived before.

TEN

It's early Monday morning and I sit on my balcony at the Breakers and watch the sunrise as I drink my coffee. I'm supposed to meet the demo crew at the house first thing. I have plenty of time to get there because first thing in Florida and first thing in New York are two very different things. First thing in New York—I already would have been late. But here in South Florida I have until nine. I'm not sure if this irks me or not. On one hand, I hate having to wait around for other people once I put my mind to accomplishing a task. On the other hand, I think I could get used to the slower timetable of the South, and don't let anyone kid you, even though people like to joke that South Florida is the fifth borough of New York, it's still very much the South. The contractor actually called me *Little Lady*. And when Michael and I met with Josè, the project manager who was assigned to our renovation, even though Michael told him point blank that I was the one he would be dealing with, he kept looking at Michael instead of me when he talked. Then he would look at me as if he suddenly remembered I was in the room, and smile and say, "Is that ok with you, ma'am?" And if I dared to speak up and ask a question, he got this puzzled look on his face. Once he even said to me, "Oh, don't worry your pretty little head over that, ma'am." Infuriating. I wanted to fire him on the spot. But Michael told me that these guys had the best reputation and that I needed to try not to overreact. I could just tell that I was not going to get along with Josè.

But now the sun is rising and it's one of those beautiful South Florida fall mornings. The humidity is suddenly gone, as if the weather gods know it's November, and I can almost feel a hint of cold in the morning air, even though it's already eighty degrees outside. The temperature will probably go up to eighty-five today, and that's just fine with me. It's already snowing up north. The ocean is calm as I look out to sea, and the waves are lapping onto the shore like an old dog licking from his water bowl, slow and content. I contemplate going for a walk along the shore but decide instead to get an early start. I'll go to the house and do a quick walk-through, take some notes, and wait for Josè.

It's seven and I'm driving over the little bridge to the mainland. Already there's rush hour traffic, but not the kind you would see in New York. Here on a Monday morning, the Jaguars, Porches, and BMWs are heading west toward I-95, on their way to work as salesmen and lawyers and such. And the Hondas, Toyotas, and small pickup trucks hauling their trailers are heading east over the bridge, to their jobs as domestics, nannies, landscapers and the like. And yes, they are actually still called domestics here.

I hang a left at Flagler and scan the blocks until I can see my new property on the corner of Granada and Flagler. Not that you could miss it, but I'm still not that familiar with the neighborhood. I pass the north corner and turn onto Valencia and park in the empty lot on the north side of the property. Just as I pull into the parking lot, I see the fox out of the corner of my eye, running from my backyard and into the yard next door. So, there really is a fox. I wonder how many there are. I'll have to ask someone about that, but not Josè. I won't give him the chance to give me that condescending look ever again by asking a stupid question.

I park the car and get out with my coffee and purse in hand and begin the long search in my purse for the keys. I'm a little concerned about that fox, and whether or not there are more, so I decide to go through the house and look for any holes in the walls or floorboards just to make sure there's no den under the house or something.

I walk into the back door by the kitchen and throw my stuff down on the only counter that wasn't damaged by the fire. It's the first time I've been back inside since the fire, and it still smells of smoke. I proceed to go through the house, making plenty of noise just in case there is a fox or any other animal in there. I want to give them plenty of time to hear me and run away. I get to the dining room with the huge fireplace in the center of the wall. Maybe they come in through the chimney? But I thought the realtor told me this fireplace had been closed up for years and no longer working.

I decide to measure the mantle and do a quick sketch. I'll have to restore it for sure, and maybe investigate reopening the chimney. I go back to the kitchen to grab my tape measure, and a pad and pencil out of my purse. Now I'm standing in front of the fireplace, with my tape measure out, pencil in my mouth, and measuring the height and width of the mantle. Next, the side panel on the left. It's a total of eight feet wide with two three-foot panels. I pull my tape out and angle it up and against one of the panels to get the height. I place my knee against the center, so I have more leverage to go up with the tape, and as I do this, I am leaning on the wall panel.

Suddenly the panel moves, and I hear a click. The wall panel is a push-latch door. A hidden room? I gently push it closed and then I push it harder this time and the door springs open. I peer inside the darkened room. It looks to be about eight feet deep, and it runs the entire length of the dining room, which is about twenty feet. I walk in and notice a faint smell of liquor and kerosene. In the dim light, I can see a bar on the right, and two barstools covered in sheets. Sitting along the back wall opposite the dining room is a settee, also covered in a sheet and a chest in front of that. The back-left wall has French doors leading out to a garden. The secret garden? Of course, but why didn't I notice that from the outside? I guess I didn't pay that much attention to it. With all that creeping fig growing over the doors, I guess I couldn't notice them from the outside.

Wow, a secret room. A speakeasy. That must be what this is, of course. The hotel was built during Prohibition. I suppose every prominent builder would include a speakeasy in their hotel.

It isn't that big, but it's big enough to entertain a few people and certainly big enough to hide the liquor. The bar is still stocked with dozens of bottles with handmade labels. There is something queer about this room though. Even though it is obviously a hidden bar whose purpose is plain to see, it is also a lady's room. I throw off the sheets and notice that the furnishings are very feminine. The red velvet settee, and the barstools to match, the carved and painted wooden chest, which is acting as a cocktail table, the old Victorian rug on the floor, even the floor lamp, which looks like an original Tiffany, are definitely feminine. This looks like a sitting room for the lady of the house. But why hide it? So strange. Was the old lady still using this room when she died? It doesn't look like it. It looks like it hasn't been touched for fifty years from the dust on the bar. Someone just closed the paneled door and walked away, and never went back. A hidden room, forgotten and abandoned. A total surprise to find, and yet I was almost expecting it, this room feels so familiar.

I open the chest. The daylight is shining in through the French doors now, just enough to see as I rummage around. There's a photo album on top. The old-fashioned kind with the black acid-free paper and the little corner pockets to hold the photos. Most of them are square, the way photos were in the 1960s, with the word Kodak printed on the back along with the date. There is a long white skirt and a bustier top, some silver flatware, two sterling silver candlesticks, some crystal—wait a second, this looks like a hope chest. But whose? The daughter's? I've heard about these things but never actually saw one. But they were a prominent family. This couldn't be the hope chest for the only child of such a prominent family, could it? I'm going to have to do some research on this family when I have some extra time, which looks very likely since it is now almost nine o'clock and Josè and the demo crew are not even here yet.

Just then I see a shadow move across the paneled door leading to the dining room. What was that? I hear people talking. I quickly close the chest and slip out of the room and I close the paneled door behind me as quietly as I can. I do not want anyone to find me here. I wonder if I could keep this room a secret and still demo the rest of the house? Just then I have the strangest feeling of déjà vu, like I have been in that room before.

"Mrs. Peters?"

Did they see me come out from behind the panel? Whose shadow was that I just saw walk by the entrance? The sound of Josè's voice is coming from the kitchen.

"Here I am, Josè." I call, as casually as I can.

"Good morning, ma'am. This is Charley. He's in charge of demo."

Charlie is a huge black man with a friendly smile and an uncharacteristically soft voice.

"Mornin', Ma'am," he says.

"Good, I have some notes here," I say with a nod to Charlie; "I don't want you to touch certain rooms of the house just yet until I've finalized my plans for the restoration." This will piss Josè off sufficiently and show him just who's the boss around here now. I walk right past Josè with a look of stupefied rejection on his face and speak, in my best lady of the house voice, directly to Charley.

"We'll start upstairs."

I proceed to walk up the grand staircase and into the first guest room with Charley following dutifully behind. There are four rooms at the front of the house, two facing the south side, and four more facing the west and the back yard below. Each room is fifteen feet long by thirteen feet wide, with French doors at the end, leading to a small private balcony, and each room has its own bathroom, which was very luxurious at the time the house was built. So, in all, the rooms were twenty feet long by thirteen feet wide and they surrounded a ten-foot-wide corridor or landing at the top of the grand stair. You cannot get into the master suite on the north side of the house from this corridor. One would have to use the back stairs off the kitchen and maid's quarters. The baths are anything but luxurious presently, but they are workable, even if small. They are five feet by six feet, with a stand-alone tub at the end of the room and a toilet and pedestal sink next to each other on one wall. There will barely be enough room to swing the door in once we replace it with the required three-foot door. Currently the doors to the bathrooms are only two feet, which is against code and also terribly uncomfortable for any grown being.

"Everything goes," I say, standing inside the first bathroom. "The tub, the sink, the water closet, and take that medicine cabinet out of the wall as well. I'll create a little niche there. Oh, and the mirrors – they go as well."

"Yes, ma'am," says Charley. "How about these light fixtures?" He asks, cupping one in his hand like a baby bird.

"No, they stay," I say.

"We'll have to tie them up and cover them, then," Charley says as he holds the baby crystal chandelier up close to the ceiling for effect.

They look like a little upside-down cup of crystals, no bigger than six inches in diameter, hanging over the old pedestal sink. I wish I could keep the sinks as well, they are quite charming, but they are too damaged. The porcelain is chipping, and the fixtures are rusted to them. The tiny pedestal tubs are also quite charming, but alas, not very user friendly, since they are really soaking tubs, you know, the kind you have to sit in with your knees bent. My guests will be expecting a modern bathroom with a shower and a rain bath showerhead.

"We will have to install shower pans in each bathroom and replace the walls with new plaster board. So, you might as well just gut the bathroom altogether. Oh, and these doors will have to be changed to three-foot doors," I tell Charley, wondering how the chandeliers will hold up during the demo. He's still standing there, gently holding it up to the ceiling.

"On second thought, Charley, take those light fixtures down and place them carefully in a storage container for reuse."

"Yes, ma'am," he says, with a satisfied look on his face.

But I pay him no more attention as I walk out of the room, thinking of finishes and fixtures. I guess I'll go shopping and see what I can find in the way of some marble tile and vanities.

I wander around the house for a while and find myself back upstairs in the master's quarters, in the sitting room on the third floor. I look out the French doors and can see clear across the island to the ocean beyond from here. What a view! I love this room, but what to do with it? I can't figure out a way to let the guests up here without going through my private quarters. I decide to keep it just as it is. A sitting room just for me, with a panoramic view and a widow's walk all around. It must be a beautiful view at night as well. And I imagine the breeze in the wintertime is fabulous. I look up and notice there is a skylight in the ceiling that has been boarded up. Must have been leaking. I make a mental note of that and walk back downstairs just in time to meet the electrician and plumber talking with my contractor, Josè.

We go over the plans for the new wiring and new plumbing, and discuss the air conditioners, which will also need ducts. Josè tells me the mechanical engineer is running late and that he'll probably be here after five, which in South Florida is code for tomorrow. I'm beginning to get used to the pace of things down here.

I skip out and leave them to their work at around noon and head over to the history museum downtown. I want to get some information about the family that used to live here.

## ELEVEN

The history museum is located on the second floor of the old courthouse, and the Historical Society of Palm Beach County is on the first floor. Great, I need to talk to someone about getting permits to renovate that pier as well. I'll kill two birds with one stone.

The courthouse itself is historical. A beautiful neo-classical structure, built in 1916 and lovingly restored in 2002, it sits among the more modern architecture of today, ugly in comparison, along the downtown corridor of Dixie Highway.

I hit the history museum first. I walk up the grand stair and into the lobby. Sitting at the front desk is none other than Daisy.

"Well, hello there! I've been expecting you," she says with a warm smile.

She is dressed up in period costume and she is using a fake British accent.

"Hello, Daisy," I say.

"No, no, no. My name is Miss Merryweather," she says in character.

"I believe you must be the new lady of the house, Miss Marina. Would you be interested in a tour of the museum? Or would you like to go straight to the archives today?"

Ok, I'll play along.

"Straight to the archives, I think."

"Very well, but first you must purchase a membership for the mere fee of fifty dollars, if you please?" still in that horrible fake accent.

"Of course," I say, as I get out my credit card and hand it to her. She seems to have no problem coming back to the present to complete the exchange of money and membership card, and then slips right back into character.

"Allow me to show you where you can find what you are looking for."

She brings me into the archives room and sits me down at a long table. The place is empty except for the two of us. She starts piling books and articles on the table, as if she had them out and ready for me. It all seems so strange. I feel like I'm trespassing on the one hand, and on the other hand I feel like I'm being played.

"I'll leave you to your work then. Please don't hesitate to ring if you have any questions. I am your neighborhood historian, and an expert on the subject at hand, you know." And with that she leaves me alone to my research.

Funny, she never mentioned the fire or even asked me how I was doing. I open the first booklet and start to read.

The entire neighborhood known as El Cid was once a pineapple plantation owned by a guy named Benjamin Lainhart back in the late 1800s. Competition from Cuba and disease soon crushed the pineapple business, so Lainhart parceled out the land. Around that time, Henry Flagler was bringing socialites down from the northern cities along his new railroad to winter at the newly built Flagler Hotel. West Palm Beach was experiencing a real estate boom in the early 1900s, and wealthy people were buying up the farmland. A socialite from Pittsburg bought all the land north of Belvedere Road and south of Flamingo Road and named it after the celebrated Spanish hero, Rodrigo Diaz de Bivar, also known as el Cid. He sold parcels to those nouveau riche riding the train down to catch the fever that was the land boom in the early 1920s, and on one of those parcels now sits my soon to be new Bed and Breakfast.

My parcel was sold to a guy named Johnny Cotton. He was a rough around the edges sort of guy from New York who made his fortune running the Flagler Hotel & Casino and later running booze to the wealthy on Palm Beach Island. He had a go-fast boat among his fleet of many and would run rum from the Bahama islands during Prohibition. He later hung out with the likes of Ernest Hemingway. He bought the property in 1920 and proceeded to build a hotel on the land.

Cheryl was only fifteen years old when she married Johnny. She was living with a wealthy Palm Beach family when he met her. She had been orphaned seven years earlier at the age of eight, when the Okeechobee Hurricane of 1928 took her parents, traveling hands from Spain, along with thousands of others. She was taken in by a prominent Palm Beach family and was educated along with their four children. Johnny took one look at her and knew she was going to be his wife. At fifteen she was already quite a beauty. She married Johnny in 1935 and moved into the hotel, along with a modest hope chest her adopted family had given her. Ah, so it must be Cheralena's hope chest that I found. Back then, society wasn't the same down south as it was in New York or Philadelphia. One could easily go from being the orphan of a farmhand to the wife of a prominent businessman. Johnny called her Cheralena, and he named the hotel Villa Cheralena after her. She ran the hotel. She did everything from greeting the socialite guests, to keeping the books, to managing the housekeepers.

Daisy pokes her head into the room, and in her British accent informs me that the museum closes at two on Mondays.

"Could you come back tomorrow?"

"Oh, sure," I say. "Thank you very much."

"I give trolley tours of the neighborhood every Friday and Saturday afternoon starting in season. I would love it if you could join me sometime."

"Thank you, I will," I say, as I walk out of the museum.

I head downstairs to the Historical Society. Wow, what history. I definitely need to get back here and read the rest of their story.

It's five o'clock when I finally leave the building and I'm exhausted. They were not nearly as friendly or organized at the Historical Society as they were at the History Museum, and I'm afraid I'm getting the runaround about the pier. First, I need to go to the preservation board and do a presentation, then I need to do another presentation in front of the residents of the neighborhood. Then the city staff makes a recommendation based on the townspeople's feedback. Then the commission puts it to a vote. Really? It's not even this complicated to put up a skyscraper in Manhattan!

Why am I hitting so many roadblocks with this project? First the fire, now this? And why does this feel so personal to me?

It's just another project, just another house.  I don't know, maybe I'm just tired.

I drive back to the Breakers and flop down on the bed. I'm hungry, angry, and tired. I realize I haven't had a thing to eat since breakfast, and as I'm thinking about calling room service, I drift off to sleep.

# TWELVE

I realize while I am sleeping that I'm having my house dream again, only this time it's different. This time I can see more detail.

*The red velvet settee, the bar on the far side of the room with the two matching barstools. I walk over to the bar and pick up a bottle of brandy. I can hear music playing in the dining room next door. I hear people laughing and talking.*

Suddenly, I bolt straight up in the bed. Oh, my God, I don't believe it. I am wide awake now. I go into the bathroom and throw some water on my face, grab my keys and head out the door.

There's a cute little restaurant on Dixie highway just a few blocks south of Southern Boulevard. I find myself driving sough along Dixie Highway on the mainland and I notice a sign all lit up in the window that reads "The Patio." There are several cars parked outside. I pull into the lot, park my car, and walk in.

The place is decorated just like someone's patio. The floors are painted concrete, and there are old stained-glass windows in their original painted wood frames hanging from fishing wire in front of the storefront windows. The seating is mostly overstuffed settees and sofas, and the tables are outdoor iron and glass. The place is hopping for nine-thirty on a Monday night during off-season. I am seated at a little glass table in the corner by the windows.

I can't think straight. I look around at the other people in the restaurant. Mostly couples and small groups, except for a very rowdy table of six in the corner of the room, obviously celebrating something, and having a good time at it. Nobody is paying any attention to me, still I feel so self-conscious.

The waitress is a very friendly-looking young girl of college age, with straight black hair and a tattoo on her left wrist that looks like a heart with a bird flying through it. She walks over and looks at me as if she recognizes me, she starts to say something, but thinks better of it.

"Hello, my name is Liz. What'll it be?"

"I'll have the homemade minestrone soup and a glass of red wine, please."

She smiles and takes my menu and walks away.

The house dream, the house dream. This is the house I've been dreaming about most of my life! My head is pounding. Think. What does this mean? What are the odds that I end up purchasing a house that I've been dreaming about most of my life? It must be a coincidence, but I know it's not. The details are too similar. I go over the dream again in my head: the red velvet settee, the bar and barstools to match, even the Tiffany lamp. They are all the same. But what does it mean? If that is the secret hiding place in my dreams, what does it mean? I've got to get back in there. I sip my soup and drink my wine.

Liz comes back to ask if I need anything else.

"Is there a hardware store open at this hour?" I ask.

"No, but there is a Walgreens open all night just over the bridge on Southern Boulevard."

"Perfect!" I say, thanking her. I pay my check and head over to Walgreens.

I'll never get used to drugstores being these mini markets. That wasn't always the case growing up in the northeast. I remember when drugstores sold drugs and first aid supplies only. But now they are like general stores. This one has everything, from bathing suits and flip-flops to beer and wine. There is a full automotive section, a hardware and housewares section, and a grocery section as well. I buy a flashlight and some batteries, and head to the house.

Back inside the house, all is quiet. It's evident the demolition has started. The first thing to do in any renovation project is to cover up all the things you want to protect. The marble floors in the ballroom are covered with brown paper, taped down at the baseboard, and there is a layer of plywood over that. The entire grand stair is covered with the same brown paper and the iron handrail is wrapped in drop cloth and heavy plastic and taped around the edges for protection. I turn on the flashlight and shine it up toward the chandelier. The chandelier has been covered with a white sheet and the shadows are playing off the walls like ghosts on the stairway. Fear creeps up into my mind. What am I doing here all alone? Suddenly, I hear a noise. What was that? Is it the fox? It's coming from the dining room. Slowly, I find my way to the dining room, sweeping the flashlight back and forth to make sure there is no fox in here with me. My knees are shaking, and my heart is pounding in my ears. Oh my God—I see another shadow! What is it? I point the flashlight up and see a flicker of light. It's just the crystal chandelier hanging in the dining room. It remains uncovered. The demo crew has left this room alone, as told. I ponder turning on the switch, but I don't dare use the electric anymore after the fire, and anyway who knows what the electrician did today.

With shaky hands, I pop open the paneled door next to the fireplace mantel. I step into the hidden room and my breath leaves my body in one quick rush. The settee, the bar, even the chest sitting on the old Victorian rug. I know this room. I lay the flashlight on the bar, pointing it toward the mirror that hangs on the wall behind it, hoping that the reflection of the light in the mirror will increase the light in the room. I look around. There is an old Victrola sitting in the corner of the bar. I step behind the bar, crank the handle, and place the needle on the record. I can't believe it's still working after all these years. Chopin is playing one of his nocturnes.

The bar is stocked with glasses that are so covered with dust that I can't even see through them. Then I look over and notice one lone snifter, sitting in the middle of the bar. Next to that is a bottle with a homemade label, and it reads: "Villa Cheralena - Private Stock, 1935." Was this here before? I don't remember noticing it. Was someone expecting me? Is that realtor still sneaking in here to cheat on his wife? But why just one glass? I pick up the glass and notice that it's clean. That's odd. I pull the cork top off the bottle and sniff it. Brandy. I pour a small amount into the glass and sniff. Smells good. I take a small sip. Tastes good. I pour myself a generous amount and take another sip. It glides down my throat and warms my entire body. I begin to relax. I walk back from behind the bar and sit myself down on one of the barstools and look at my reflection in the mirror. I don't recognize myself. Oh sure, I see my long, wavy black hair, and the white dress I am wearing, but the girl looking back at me from the mirror isn't me. I walk over to the settee with the bottle of brandy in one hand and the snifter in the other. I put the bottle down on the side table and sit down. I've got to calm my nerves.

As I sip the brandy and listen to Chopin, I think about Halloween and all that has happened since then. The fire seems like it happened a year ago now. And Michael seems like a stranger. It's only been two days, but we haven't spoken since he left and I'm uneasy with the way we left things. I take another sip of brandy. Oh, well. I don't really mind being here all alone as much as I thought I would. Who needs him anyway, with his bossy stubbornness and his negative attitude? I can handle this on my own, and in fact I'd rather be alone. I kind of like the feeling of being by myself in this room. This room feels special to me, like I'm home. I put my feet up on the chest and pour myself another glass of brandy. The strangeness of being in this room after all these years of dreaming about it is melting away with each sip of brandy. I can remember the feeling I had in the dream of feeling safe in here and not wanting to leave here, ever.

The moonlight slips out from behind a cloud and is shining through the French doors now, and in the garden outside. It's lovely in here with the moonlight casting shadows onto the walls. I have the strangest feeling that I'm not alone. The shadows are filling the space around me now, like old friends come to visit. I find myself thinking about the women who lived here. Cheralena, what was she like? And Cheralena's daughter, what was she like? Did she really commit suicide or was it an accident? Why would anyone be sad or lonely in such a lovely place as this? And who is the ghost that is supposed to be haunting this house? Is it the daughter? Or is it someone else from another time? Mozart's *Requiem* is playing softly on the Victrola now and I drift off to sleep. A nice, peaceful sleep. The kind of sleep I haven't had in a long time.

*She's playing in the garden while her mother is planting her flowers and tending to her vegetables. It's a lovely fall day and she is humming a little tune she learned in school. The morning air is cool, and the sun is not too hot yet. There is a light breeze blowing through the trees. All the sudden her mother looks up with a worried look on her face. She is looking at a man standing across the street with his hands in his pockets. He looks right at her. He looks very sad and then hangs his head down, he's looking at something on his shoes. Her mother grabs her arm and hurries her into the house. What? What did I do wrong? Why do I have to go inside? "Is that man mad at us, mother? Is he going to hurt us?" She shushes the girl and hurries her into the secret room and shuts the door and locks it.*

Suddenly I'm awake. Did I just hear something? I sit very still and hold my breath. There's something moving outside in the garden. I must have fallen asleep and was dreaming. I get up slowly and walk over to the French doors and look outside. There's nothing there. I check the time on my phone, it's 5:00 a.m. My head is killing me. I'd better get out of here before the workers show up and find me here.

I slip out the paneled door and find my way through the dining room and back to the kitchen entrance. I make my way to my car in the moonlight, careful not to run into the fox, or whatever it was that I just heard in the garden. I get in the car and I head back to the Breakers. The moon is low in the western sky but still bright enough to throw light onto the water as I drive over the bridge. It's beautiful and serene, the water below the bridge, rippling lightly with the outgoing tide.

Luckily there's nobody in the lobby when I get back to the hotel, and I head straight up to my room without being seen. What a mess I am. My hair is a mess, my clothes are all dirty from sitting in that dusty room, and I feel like death. I take a shower and get dressed for the day. My head is pounding. Why did I drink that brandy? I head down to the café to grab some coffee and something to eat. What was that dream I was having? I can't remember, but I think it had something to do with the secret garden.

There is a nice little courtyard with a fountain in the middle and tables scattered around it, just outside the coffee shop at the Breakers. There is no one here at this hour and I am glad to have the place to myself.

Today I am going to find another place to stay. The Breakers is nice, but too expensive. I can't live here all year. And I want a kitchen, so I don't have to eat out every night. I'll look for a little efficiency on the mainland.

I grab the local newspaper and order a cup of coffee and a muffin and walk out into the courtyard. I sit at one of the tables by the fountain and sip my coffee as I browse through the real estate rentals. The water in the fountain reminds me of the water rippling under the bridge. What was it about that water under the bridge? And what was that dream I was having? Lingering memories, too faint for me to conjure up now, tug at me as I try to concentrate on the morning paper.

## THIRTEEN

I find a little cottage on Cordova Road, just west of Olive. I can't believe how much the rentals go up for the season around here, and I really feel lucky to have found this cottage. The landlord is a heavy-set woman with a broad face and a warm smile. She greets me at the front door of the main house with a firm handshake and tells me her name is Lucy. She is a retired schoolteacher, whose children have grown up and moved away. She lives all alone now (I didn't ask her where her husband is) and is very picky about her seasonal rentals. She shows me around the place, talking a mile a minute, like we're old friends catching up. I instantly like her, but I don't know if I should keep my distance or not. I know how meddlesome some people can be, especially lonely empty nesters with nothing else to do. So, I remain polite but elusive. Occasionally she stops mid-sentence and looks at me as if to say, "Do I know you?" and then continues on, talking a mile a minute.

The cottage is a small one-bedroom, one-bath stand-alone guest house with a small kitchen and a private drive behind the main house. It's furnished in a beachy, shabby chic, and it's perfect for me. I compliment Lucy on her decorating skills and her eyes light up like a child. There is a little fenced yard around the cottage, and a private driveway so I'll have total privacy. I especially like that it's separate from the main house because I don't want to have to run into Lucy every day and be invited in for tea or something. And the best part is, I'm right around the corner from Villa Cheralena, so I could walk there if I needed to. We agree on a month-to-month lease and I thank her for her time. I can move in right away, she tells me, and hands me a key.

Before I turn to leave, I find myself stopping and asking, "Tell me something Lucy, do you believe in ghosts?" I don't know why I just asked her that.

"You mean, Marina?"

"Who's Marina?" I ask.

"Don't you know? She was Cheralena's daughter, the original owner of your new house, the one who was killed in the storm."

"Was it an accident, or did she kill herself?"

"No one knows for sure, but they say she died before her time. That's why she comes back to haunt. She has unfinished business."

"I think people who say they see ghosts are crazy, don't you?" I ask, trying to sound casual.

"You don't have to worry about me, honey," she says. "I won't think you're crazy. I have my own ghosts to contend with, so don't you worry."

I suddenly regret asking her, and I feel foolish even talking about it, so I just thank her awkwardly and turn to go. Just then the fox appears from behind the bushes.

"There, there," Lucy says, as she bends down and holds her hand out as if she is calling a stray cat, oh wait, it *is* a cat. A huge orange tabby. So there really is no fox living in this neighborhood.

"I thought that cat was a fox when I saw her the other day," I say.

"There are no foxes in this area anymore, although they used to live in these parts years ago," Lucy replies. "They were considered good luck, but then people started hunting them and they finally died out," she says. "I think she might be getting ready to have a litter. I usually never see her show herself in broad daylight. I leave a little bowl of milk out for her at night, just in case."

She's treating that stray like a pet. I hope she knows what she's doing. Oh well, maybe she's a little eccentric, but she's still a nice lady. And at least I know I'm not crazy now.

I've decided to return the rental car and get a lease. Might as well, since I'll be here for a year. I get a great deal on a little red convertible Mini Cooper. I really feel like I'm a "Palm Beacher" now, and I drive all around town with the top down. Even though it's December it's still 80 degrees outside. I'm wondering when it's going to get cold, if ever?

I also went shopping in the local vintage clothing store and bought some more suitable clothes to wear. I can't believe I came down here with all these dark suits and high heels. I can't be dressing like I'm going to work in New York City anymore, it just isn't suitable. So I purchased some long, lightweight cotton skirts and blouses. It feels so much better to not have to wear stockings and shoes anymore either. I just throw on a long skirt and a pair of sandals and put my hair up in a ponytail. And I never wear makeup anymore, why should I? It's much more natural this way, not to mention easier.

Villa Cheralena is a mess, and it looks depressing. The kitchen is totally gutted. The cabinets are torn out from the walls and piled up in the center of the room. The new cabinets are on order, with a twelve-week lead time, which should give the contractors enough time to finish the electrical and plumbing work. The yellow and white daisy wallpaper is stripped off the walls, exposing black mold and gaping holes underneath. There are holes in the ceiling where the new lighting will go. I'm having a hard time getting the mechanical engineer to show up. I don't know what his problem is, and José is being no help at all. Now that season is approaching, he is busy working on the island, preparing the multi-million-dollar mansions in anticipation of the snowbirds' arrival. He and his crew are spread too thin, and I am not getting the attention I have become accustomed to. Oh well, at least the demo crew is still here, working every day. They are grinding down the heavy plaster on the walls. There is enough dust being kicked up to kill a small army. I'm worried about those men, working in all that dust without masks on. And I wonder about the lead in the old paint.

I've decided to stay away during the day, fearing all that dust is what is causing these terrible headaches. I return in the afternoons to check on progress and answer any questions.

Michael has called exactly three times, always informing me that he can't break away from his all-important job and his all-important life. I assure him that it's ok. He doesn't have to come until the town meeting for the pier approval. I don't want him here anyway. He'd only get in my way. I spend my days shopping for furniture, fixtures, and finishes for the house. I'm almost finished selecting everything for the guest rooms and the master suite. All I have left is the public spaces on the ground floor and the observation room on the third floor.

And I've cleaned up Cheralena's parlor. I pulled the sheets off the furniture and cleaned them, polished the floors and cleaned the windows leading to the garden. I even washed the clothes that were in the chest and hung them up in my closet with my things. At first I felt like an intruder, going to Cheralena's secret room, but I'm getting over that feeling now. After all, I am the new owner, am I not? Sometimes I go to that room for solitude in the evenings. It feels nice to be there alone with her things.

Last weekend I worked in the garden. I pulled out all the dead flowers in the planters and planted bright pink geraniums and blue hyacinths, and I trimmed the creeping fig vines on the wall. There's a little marble plaque lying in the corner of the garden with the inscription "Marina" on it and nothing else. I wonder if it's her headstone, but why no dates? I polished it and planted some lavender and wildflowers behind it. I also cleaned and filled the fountain and plugged it in, and to my surprise it works. I just can't find the key to open the gate, though, so I had to bring everything around from the kitchen entrance. I guess I'll have to get that lock cut eventually, but for now it's ok. I'm not going anywhere; I could spend all day in that garden anyway.

Lucy has been really nice to me. Every time she sees me, she invites me into her house. I think she thinks I'm lonely, living here all alone, but I'm not really. I've decided to invite her to lunch tomorrow to thank her for being so kind.

We're going to The Patio, that same restaurant I went to the other night. Evidently, it's the best place in town.

"Hi Lucy!" It's the same waitress, the one with the tattoo, who greets us at the door with menus. "Your usual table?" she asks.

"That would be great, thanks Liz," Lucy says with a warm smile.

"Oh, hi!" Liz says to me with a look of excitement on her face. "I just knew you were," she hesitates, and for just a second I think I see Lucy give her a look, "I knew you were going to be a regular," she continues. "I just knew I would see you again, that's all. Welcome," she says awkwardly and turns around quickly, bowing her head slightly so as not to catch Lucy's eye as she leads us to the table.

"What was that all about?" I ask Lucy, when Liz leaves with our drink orders.

"Oh, that's nothing," Lucy assures me. "She's just a little kooky, that's all."

Liz comes back with our iced teas and takes our lunch order. She seems a little disappointed now, like she did something wrong and was scolded for it. Funny girl. One minute she's ecstatic to see me, like we're old friends, and the next minute she won't even look at me. Oh well. Lunch arrives and it is delicious. The atmosphere in here is so serene. No wonder this is the most popular place in town. I am really enjoying myself. I guess I need to get out more often and socialize with actual people.

During lunch, Lucy tells me all about her life. Her two sons have gone off to college, and as soon as they were out of the house her cheating husband left her for a younger woman.

"I knew he was cheating on me all along. But I never thought he would actually leave me," she says.

"I would see her in the neighborhood, driving by the house on the weekends. She worked at the local gym. Yoga instructor or something. She was one of those Barbie types. Young, beautiful blonde with a perfect body. I knew I could never compete with that. But I always thought it was just a fling. You know, mid-life crisis or something. I waited for him to get over it. I never confronted him. I always thought we had something more than that. Something stronger, you know? We were married for 25 years when he left. He didn't say much that day. He just told me that he didn't love me anymore and that he was leaving. Then he packed his clothes and walked out."

Gee, that's so sad, I think to myself.

"Just like that. No explanation, no marriage counseling, no argument, not even an apology. As if it was my fault he no longer loved me. I still haven't forgiven him. I signed the divorce papers when they came. What else could I do? He left me everything, the house, the bank account. There was nothing to fight about. But I'll never forgive him just the same. I think that's the worst part about it. We never fought. I never got to tell him how angry I was. I was left here all alone with my anger and no one to tell it to. No way to let it out. Just a closed door in my face."

I reach across the table and put my hand on hers in sympathy. She looks like she's going to cry, but she doesn't. She just sips her iced tea and smiles at me.

After a few minutes, in her cheery voice she says, "Shall we do some antique shopping?"

This part of Dixie Highway is known as Antique Row. Up and down the tree lined street are shops with new and used furniture and accessories. I can't resist.

"Well, I'd love to," I say. I pay the tab against Lucy's protest, and we walk out into the sunshine. The shops are full of tourists and decorators, and every store owner knows Lucy by name. I buy some lovely things for the house. An antique dining room set that seats twenty that cost me a little fortune, but I just can't resist. It looks like it belongs in my dining room, and probably did at some point. Some Queen Anne chairs and a settee for my bedroom. The shop owner promises to hold the furniture until I am ready for delivery, free of charge. Everyone is being so warm and friendly to me. I don't know if it's because I am with Lucy or because I told them I was going to open Villa Cheralena again. Any new business in town is always good for the existing businesses. I am invited to come back in the spring when they hold their annual block party and advertise my new bed and breakfast in several of the shops.

Every spring Antique Row closes off to vehicle traffic and holds a huge block party, with food and drinks and strolling musicians. They mark down all the items that didn't move during season. It's the last hurrah before summer, when the snowbirds go back up north, and the tourists all go home, and business slows to a crawl. Some of the shops also close for the off-season, and the proprietors go up to Newport or the Hamptons and open their summer shops.

We're walking out of a lighting store and Lucy takes me by the elbow.

"There's someone I want you to meet. Her name is Agnus. She's a fixture in this town and an expert on antiques. Anything you want to know; you just ask Agnus. She probably even knows who owned it originally. She has lived here all her life, and she knows everybody and everything about this town. Her shop is right next door."

We walk into a tiny little shop called Lost Treasures. It's full of antique jewelry and tabletop accessories. Some items are new, hostess-type gifts, and some are homemade items, but most are antiques. Out of the back comes the most exquisite black woman I've ever seen. She's tall and thin, and she's wearing an emerald green silk caftan. She has a head scarf of every color imaginable piled high on her head and she is wearing large gold hoop earrings. She looks to be in her 70s, but there's not a wrinkle on her face, and her eyes are just as emerald as her dress.

She walks, no—she glides toward us, and with outstretched arms she takes me by both hands. She looks me in the face so intently, I think I blush a little.

"Agnus, this is Teresa," Lucy says, "She is restoring Villa Cheralena."

"Of course she is," Agnus says to Lucy, and then turns back to me and says, "Welcome home, my dear. I have something for you. I've been waiting a long time to give it to you."

What a strange thing to say. I'm feeling a little intimidated, like she knows some deep secret of mine and she is threatening to give it away.

She comes back out with a small wooden box and places it in my hands. It's no bigger than a cigar box, and it's made of richly carved dark mahogany, with ivory and ebony inlay.

"How beautiful," I say, as I inspect the intricate pattern. I open it and out comes Brahms' *Lullaby*. A music box. Inside the red velvet interior lies an antique key attached to a long, black velvet ribbon.

"This belongs to the house and I want you to have it."

"Oh no, I couldn't possibly—"

"Please, I insist."

I do as I'm told and take the box.

"What does the key belong to?" I ask.

"I want you to come back and visit me. Do you promise? Come back and visit me when you find where the key belongs, ok?"

"Sure," I say, and with that Lucy tells me she must get going. So, we say our goodbyes and head out the door.

"Strange woman. What did she mean, she's been waiting for me?" I ask.

"Oh, I never worry too much about what Agnus says. I just do what I'm told." Lucy laughs. "She's a good person to know in this town. Especially if you need to get anything done by way of the Historic Board. She's like our unofficial mayor. No, actually she's more like the Godmother of El Cid. She knows how to get people to do things. You'll see."

Later that night I find myself back at the house. I let myself into Cheralena's parlor and sit down at the bar. I open the music box and listen again to Brahms' *Lullaby*. Suddenly, I have an overwhelming urge to have another glass of that brandy. I sit there for some time fingering the key on its velvet ribbon and contemplating if I should take that drink. That's strange, I don't remember washing that snifter out after I was in here last time, but there it is. A single clean snifter sitting in the middle of the bar, next to the bottle of brandy like it was waiting to welcome me home. I pour myself a glass. The warm liquid burns slightly as it travels down to my stomach, warming me to the bone. I don't know why I hesitated in the first place to have this drink. Or why I hesitated to take the music box from Agnus, or buy this house for that matter. It feels so right, like home. I look outside at the pink clouds in the west and then back to my reflection in the mirror behind the bar.

For a second, I don't recognize myself. Who is that girl staring back at me? She looks like me, but the eyes aren't mine. I take the key out of the music box again and I roll it around in my hand. It's an old-fashioned skeleton key. The kind that fits into an antique padlock.

That's it! I jump up and go out to the garden, and sure enough the key fits. I turn the lock on the gate and it opens. Great, now I won't have to cut the lock. I lock the gate and go back inside and hang the key on a hook behind the bar. It's all coming together now. It's all falling neatly into place. I can feel her eyes on me, that girl in the mirror.

I get up and go sit on the settee. I open the hope chest and start rummaging through it. What's this? It looks like a diary. I don't remember seeing that in here before either. Oh well, it's here now, so I might as well read it. I open the book and flip through the pages. Yes, it is a diary. It looks like it's Cheralena's diary. I flip back to the first page and start reading Cheralena's life story, and what a fascinating story it is.

# FOURTEEN

*March 25, 1935*

*Cheralena, he calls me. He's building me a grand house and he's going to name it after me! Villa Cheralena. I'm going to be a lady, a married lady. Papa wasn't too keen on the idea at first, but that old witchy wife of his insisted he either marry me off or get out of her house. Can you imagine that? That old witch is jealous of me? Me! I have nothing, and she has everything, and she's jealous — why? Just because Papa calls me up to his rooms at night and not her, that's why. But I'm sure she wouldn't do the things to him that he makes me do, why would she? She's a proper lady, she doesn't have to do those things to get by. Me, I don't care really, I get stuff back in return. I get nice dresses and I get to go to parties, and now this. Now I'm gonna get married to Johnny Cotton. Now I'm gonna be a lady too.*

*The wedding's gonna be in June, and Papa's going to give me away, just like a real father. And I'm gonna have a white wedding gown, and a big party, and presents too! Those brats have to be in my wedding party, but who cares? Once it's over and I move out, move into my own house with my own husband, I won't ever have to see those brats again.*

*He's taking me to Paris on our honeymoon. He's so rich. We're gonna have the main stateroom on the nicest steamship there is, The Queen Victoria.*

*He showed me pictures, it's even nicer than this old dump. And when we come back, the house will be finished. My house, my very own house, with maids and a butler! I'll show those brats and that witchy wife who never even liked me, never even let me call her mother, or mum, or even auntie. I'll show those witches. I'll throw the biggest parties and I won't ever invite them!*

But that's not exactly how it went. Oh, Cheralena got married all right, and Johnny Cotton was rich, even more wealthy than Cheralena's adopted father. And they did go to Paris on their honeymoon. But Johnny Cotton was a gangster, and he was a womanizer, and it wasn't long before Cheralena was in the shoes of the bitter wife while her husband was fooling around with other women, young beautiful women. The first was a hostess on the Queen Victoria, while on the way to Paris for their honeymoon. And then there was a procession of fancy women while they were in Paris. But Cheralena kept herself busy shopping for the latest fashions and things for the house. She didn't seem to mind. She desperately wanted to have a baby though. Thinking that would solidify her standing in the marriage and fill the void in her life, but it seemed that was not in the cards either.

By the time they got back to the states, the house was finished and Cheralena was the talk of the town. They threw lavish parties, and Cheralena wore the beautiful clothes, the latest fashions she bought in Paris, and she wore a five-carat diamond ring on her finger. But there was no love in that marriage, and no love making either, just sex, dirty sex. The kind of sex she was used to having with Papa since she was just a girl. The kind of sex she had learned early on could open doors and get her places and allow her to survive in this cruel world. The only kind of sex she knew. And soon she stopped that too. She found out she didn't have to say yes anymore, now that she was legally married. She could just lock the bedroom door, or pretend she was asleep, and Johnny would just go elsewhere. He didn't even seem to mind. It became clear to Cheralena that all Johnny really wanted was someone to manage the house and throw the parties and count the money. And that was just fine with her. The only regret she had was that she never did have that baby she wanted so badly. Maybe she couldn't get pregnant, or maybe it was Johnny, she didn't know.

It seems that Mr. Cotton was running an illegal casino right here in this very house. Throwing lavish parties for wealthy Palm Beachers and hosting high-stakes poker games in the dining room. Yes, the room with only one window facing the street. It all makes perfect sense to me now. And when the law showed up, they could easily hide the cash and the cards in the secret parlor. He was also running a brothel. Using the guest rooms upstairs for his ladies to entertain the rich, fat husbands whose wives were too high class to venture over the bridge and associate with the common folk on the mainland. And as for Cheralena, well, she was the one managing the place. I learned that this was her private parlor and even Johnny wasn't allowed in. Yes, she knew all right that Johnny was upstairs with the whores at night, but she didn't care, as long as she had her own private parlor that she could go to. There was mention of a cash box, buried out in the garden in its own miniature grave, where no one could find it. No one that is, but the lady of the house. One day the police came to raid the place and found nothing but Cheralena working in her garden. I wonder if that's when it was walled off. Critters indeed!

And then the war started. Every man under thirty years old had suddenly gone off to war. Johnny Cotton's casino business must have slowed down considerably, but he continued to run the brothel. And they continued to have parties in the ballroom and play poker in the dining room. The men were mostly older Palm Beach society. The townspeople knew what was going on and they were furious, but they could never prove it. They tried several times to shut it down, but each time there was a raid, Cheralena would usher the men into her secret parlor, and they would hide out there until the police left. But soon they stopped coming for fear of getting caught and ruining their reputations.

Then the sailors arrived. Only these sailors were not Americans. These sailors were the enemy. They would sneak ashore at night and take comfort with the girls. This was a much different crowd. These were boys, really, some not more than seventeen years old. They missed their mothers and their homeland. They were quiet and shy, and very polite, and they were mostly Italians. They reminded Cheralena of her own people from Spain. She liked them much better than the rough and rowdy crowd of the old, privileged class that she and her husband used to entertain. Johnny didn't mind that they were the enemy. They're Italian, just like him, after all. And their money's green. So, he let Cheralena host their little parties while he went out drinking with his friends.

She especially liked one of them very much. He spoke English and they got to know each other well. He would come to visit her every night and she would feed him home-cooked meals. One night he brought her a Victrola and some records. They stayed up until the wee hours of the morning, just talking and listening to music. In the morning, he went back to his U-Boat off the coast of Palm Beach.

Another entry reads:

*January 15, 1942*

*The sailors came ashore again last night. They are very shy and extremely polite. Some of them speak a little English and the one named Geo speaks English very well. He explained to me that they are not fighters. They are Italian after all, and Italians are lovers – not fighters. They are just patrolling the coastline, and their main duty is to report any military activity. They really don't want to fight the Americans. They really don't even want to be in this war at all, but most of them had no choice. They secretly hate the Germans. The German officers treat them like slaves. They are considered low-class workers and nothing more. The Germans think they are superior to the Italians as a race, and they are just using Mussolini for manpower. The Italians, being mostly farmers and sons of farmers, are not literate, most of them. Geo is very smart, though. He can read and write in Italian, German, and English. He is the oldest, at 19, and sort of the unofficial leader of the group. I asked him where his commander was, and he told me the officers mostly stay on the ship and just surface to let the lower-class seamen out onto their inflatables at night. They go ashore and steal supplies, and spy on the Americans. Sometimes the officers also go ashore on the Island.*

*But Geo and his fellow seamen are tired of spying on the Americans. They have been away from home for too long, and they are lonely and homesick. Most of them were taken from their families as young boys and forced to join the military. Some of them have not seen their mothers for years.*

*They are very appreciative of the girls and very respectful, though I know they are getting more than just companionship from them when they go up to the rooms with them at night. They pay their money, and that's ok with me, if that's ok with the girls. These men, boys really, are not our enemy. I enjoy their company and the house feels joyful for once.*

*Geo never goes upstairs with the girls and the other men. He stays downstairs with me in my parlor. Johnny's always out drinking with his buddies anyway. It's nice to have someone pay special attention to me. And someone my own age. We sit and listen to classical music on the Victrola and sip my husband's brandy. Geo knows all about music. He is very well educated. I must remember to ask him where he was schooled next time I see him. I hope there is a next time.*

Then one night, her sailor came to her and they made love for the first time. She had never known love like this before. Her husband was a cold, hard man and much older than she. He treated her more like a whore than a wife, showing her how to please him in bed and never really thinking to please her. But this boy was different. He caressed her and kissed her all over her body. He would whisper sweet things to her and moan softly in her ear. He told her he loved her. Afterward, as they lay in each other's arms, they talked about running away. Just the two of them, starting over in some other town, some other state.

Meanwhile, Johnny Cotton and his friends, Ernest Hemmingway included, would go out drinking all night and then take to their boats, like little boys playing cowboys and Indians. Bored, wealthy old men whose only other pastime was fishing, looking for a little adventure, now turned lookouts for the government. Not that they really cared about the war, you see.

These men were just out looking for adventure, patrolling the coastline in their fishing boats until the early morning hours. Afterward they would go drinking at Taboo' with the very captains they had just been chasing. It was like big game fishing on the water, but in the bar, they were all very friendly, buying rounds of drinks for each other.

Until of course the night Johnny Cotton died;

*February 5th., 1943*

*I lost my husband today. I can't believe he's gone. He went out last night with his friends to patrol the waters and now he's gone, just like that. I am a widow at 22. But I don't feel like grieving. I'm too angry to grieve. How am I going to survive?*

What happened to him after that I don't know, because there are pages missing. A whole section neatly torn out, like someone wanted those pages gone, but also wanted to preserve them.

It's late and I'm getting sleepy now. There is a crescent moon shining in through the French doors leading to the garden. Michael's coming in tomorrow to give the presentation to the city for the marina. He wants me to go home with him for Christmas. I don't want to go, but I guess I'll have to. Perhaps I'll bring the diary to keep me company.

I pack up my things and walk back to my cottage for the night. Someone is following me. I hear movement in the bushes. I look over my shoulder and see something darting in and out of the brush, but I'm not afraid. It's probably just that stray cat. As I lay in bed, I hear someone crying softly in the distance. I wonder if it's Lucy missing her husband.

## FIFTEEN

The feeling of dread wakes up before me this morning. I had that dream of being in the cemetery again last night. When I awoke, it was 2:00 a.m. and I couldn't sleep anymore, so I went for a walk. I walked to the cemetery on Dixie Highway and found myself retracing my steps in the dream. I don't know what I thought I would find there, but I just walked up and down the rows of headstones for hours. Then I came back home and went back to bed.

I guess I've realized all along that I have been dreaming of this place. This house, this street, the graveyard. Who am I looking for in there? Finally, I give up trying to figure it out and get myself ready for the day.

The contractors are tearing down the walls in the bathrooms today and exposing the old leaky plumbing underneath. The studs are rotted and need to be replaced before we can install new pipes and plaster board for the shower surround. The old doors are gone and they're hacking through the lath and plaster to widen the openings. There is dust everywhere. I can't even go upstairs, it's so bad. But the ground floor demo is finally finished. They sanded the heavy plaster off the walls and are smooth-coating them. We did the demolition from the bottom up and we'll do the rebuild from the top down. Soon, we'll have a fresh coat of paint on the new walls, and new crown molding in the guest rooms. And new Carrera marble on the floors in the bathrooms. The windows are on order, as are the fixtures for the bathrooms. The original hardwood floors in the bedrooms will be sanded and stained last thing. Then we'll move down to the first floor and install the new kitchen and powder room fixtures. And finally, re-finish the marble floors and grand stair. Everything is pretty much on schedule. We just have to get that permit for the Marina and we'll be in good shape.

We're sitting at the town hall meeting with our contractor José. It's cold and raining outside, and my feet are still wet from stepping in puddles while running in the rain in my black business suit and pumps, to get here at six. It's now ten and I'm hungry and tired, and they're still going on and on about safety, and traffic and vagrants, and why don't we just demolish that pier anyway? It was never safe after all.

Do they hate the idea of me having a pier when they can't have one? Do they hate me? Or do they just hate change of any kind? We have the riparian rights to that pier! I found an old photograph at the history museum of how the pier used to look, and Michael's taken great pains to restore the original look. Even going so far as to finding the original specs on the lamp posts and having them duplicated. He is standing up in front of the room with his rendering on an easel, patiently trying to explain this to the crowd.

I'm sitting in the front row looking straight ahead while, one by one, my good neighbors, who haven't given me eye contact or even bothered to come up and introduce themselves to us, step up to the podium with their notes in hand, and proceed to give hateful speeches as to why we shouldn't be able to do this. Then they start arguing with the city council about the bed and breakfast, which is not even on the agenda, and is grandfathered in anyway. It is clear they don't want us to open a bed and breakfast in their neighborhood, and it is clear they don't want us in this town, period. I'm getting angry, and it's all I can do to keep from standing up and giving them a piece of my mind. Michael is being his usual calm, polite self, and I'm starting to resent him for it.

They actually believe the house is really haunted! Are we living in the eighteenth century? They sound like they're about to have a witch hunt, and I believe I am the witch they want to burn at the stake.

My only two friends—Daisy, my crazy neighbor in the orange house, and Lucy—are sitting together in the back of the room, silently supporting me, but not saying a word out loud on my behalf. I don't really blame them. I wonder where Agnus is. I guess

I should have called her. Maybe she doesn't know about this meeting, or maybe she can't be bothered. I never did go back to see her like I promised.

It's clear to me that we're going to have to hire a lawyer to get the final approval for the B&B. After all the work I've put into this house so far, I am not about to give up now. This house is in my blood now, its history, like the ever-present dust, a part of me. I am not giving up.

The meeting is finally over and our good neighbors file out one by one into the rain. Michael and I wait for the last ones to leave the room before we head out to the lobby. Daisy and Lucy are waiting for us there.

"You won't forget to come to the neighborhood Christmas party, now, will you?" Daisy asks in her little girl voice.

"Oh, no. We won't forget," I lie, as we proceed to run out into the rainy night.

Michael helps me into his car and we drive east over the bridge toward the Breakers in silence. He insisted on staying at the Breakers, saying my little cottage, although cute for me, is nevertheless too small for the both of us. I don't think he likes Lucy, and I don't think Lucy likes him very much either. There was a weird moment when I introduced them earlier today, as if they had known each other in some past life, and they were enemies. Maybe she just hates all men now, after what her husband did to her.

"Well, that went well," he finally says with a chuckle, trying to break the gloom of silence by being funny.

"Oh yeah. Just terrific," I say, sarcastically. I wonder what's wrong with me? Why can't I remember why I loved this man so much such a short time ago? Why don't I want to be here with him? We are driving in silence now, past the rows of majestic palm trees on either side of the long drive that leads to the front of the Breakers. I wish I had a different life. I wish I could have dinner parties with friends again. Laughing and acting crazy, like when we were young. There's no excitement in my life anymore. I feel like I'm waiting at the train station, but the train never comes. The rain is pounding on the windshield like the migraine in my temples.

"Ah, civilization," Michael says, opening the door to our hotel room. He puts his arms around my waste and gives me that look that I know so well.

"Not tonight, Michael. I have a splitting headache and I just want to lie down," I say, which is true. He lets me go with a grunt, flops down on the bed and turns on the news.

Tomorrow, we head to New York for the holidays. I don't feel very festive. I lay awake all night, thinking about Cheralena and her lover, and wishing I had romance in my life again.

## SIXTEEN

New York City feels cold and dirty to me, and Michael is acting cold and distant. He says I've changed. I guess I have. I'm miserable up here and I want to go home. I realize I am thinking of Florida and Villa Cheralena as home for the first time. I'm standing in the middle of my apartment on the Upper West Side, looking around the room like it's someone else's house. It seems foreign to me now, with all the dark furniture and the heavy draperies. I envision my new ballroom with its black and white marble floor, the crystal chandeliers hanging from the decorative plastered ceiling. Smooth white walls, long white sheer draperies blowing in the gentle breeze, coming in through the opened French doors. Sunlight all around. That's where I want to spend my Christmas. Not this cold, dark, dreary place. Oh well, next year. I'll have to buy a grand piano for the ballroom. Maybe I'll go see Agnus when I get back and ask her where I can get one.

Carly's coming tonight for Christmas Eve dinner. My only ray of sunshine. She's bringing a young man she met at school. His name is James. We have reservations at Michelangelo's and then at the Starlight Ballroom for cocktails and dancing. What was Michael thinking, making reservations there on Christmas Eve? It's going to be packed with tourists. I dread it. The night drags on. I don't feel much like dancing and sit out most of the night like a widowed grandmother at a wedding, watching Carly and James together on the dancefloor. I like him, and I can tell they really like each other as well. He looks at her the way Michael used to look at me when we were young and first in love. Michael is dancing for the fifth time with some woman from the office, Sheila, whom I never liked. She's a bleached blonde with fake boobs and she's here with the girls from accounting, who are also sitting out this dance, but unlike me they're giggling and carrying on like teenagers while they're watching the dancefloor. Sheila's boobs are bouncing up and down, almost coming out of her low-cut Valentino knock-off. I don't care. Let him have his fun, they're fake anyway. All I have to do is get through these next two days and then I can go home again. Michael's mad at me for not staying until New Year's Eve. I gave him the excuse that I don't feel good enough to go to the big, yearly office party, and besides I have nothing to wear. My New York clothes don't fit me anymore, they're all too big, and besides I hate the look of them.

I get up to go to the Ladies room for something to do. I'm sick of watching my husband and those fake boobs on the dancefloor.

"Another glass of champagne, please", I tell the bartender on my way out the door, and he obliges. I down the bubbly in one long gulp, not even tasting it and the glass slips out from my fingers just as I pass through the double doors. It smashes onto the marble floor in the grand hall. "oh shit, I'm drunk", I say to myself as I slip on the wet floor and land on my knees, and a piece of broken glass pierces my skin just below the hem of my cocktail dress.

Shit, time to get up and scurry into the ladies' room before somebody sees me, oh but too late.

"What the hell are you doing?" Michael demands.

"I'm going to the ladies' room".

"On your hands and knees? Teresa, you're drunk!"

No shit, Sherlock

He comes over and grabs my elbow a little too forcefully and pulls me up on my wobbly legs.

"Leave me alone", I realize I'm slurring my words. How did I get so drunk on three glasses of champagne? I guess I should have eaten dinner. He pulls me into the vestibule by the bathrooms and he's yelling at me in a very loud whisper, something incoherent. All I can think of is I hope Carly doesn't come out and see us. We must look a dreadful sight. I can feel the blood trickling down my calf, and I let out a chuckle. What would Cheralena do in this situation? She would probably just turn and walk away as if he weren't even there, and so I try to do just that, but Michael still has me by the arm.

"I thought you didn't feel well?"

"I don't," I mumble.

"Then why are you getting drunk and causing a scene in front of the girls from accounting?"

"The girls from accounting? What does that mean? Who gives a damn about the girls from accounting?", I'm screaming now, so Michael shoves me into the ladies' room, which is miraculously empty, and locks the door behind us. I look in the mirror and my face looks green in the fluorescent lights and my mascara is smudged because for some reason I'm crying now, but I can't remember why.

"What the hell is wrong with you, Teresa?" He's on bended knee with a wet paper towel and is wiping the blood from my leg.

It all looks so bizarre from where I stand, looking into the mirror at some cartoonish monster version of me, and Michael on his knee like he's proposing, but in an angry way. I start to laugh again. Just a giggle at first, but then a long hearty laugh escapes my throat.

"That's it. You're going home." He says.

"Oh, now that's convenient. Just call me a cab and send me home so you can go fuck Sheila tonight. Well, I have news for you – I don't care. Merry Christmas."

"This isn't an excuse to sleep with Sheila", he says. "I could have slept with her any time I wanted to while you were down in Florida doing God knows what."

"Go ahead then. See what I care."

"You know I don't want to sleep with Sheila. You know I want you to stay until New Year's Eve."

"Well, I don't want to stay until New Year's Eve," I say. Maybe he will spend the night with Sheila, I really don't care.

"I don't want to spend my New Year's Eve drinking with a bunch of people that I have nothing in common with anymore. I quit that job months ago and haven't spoken to one of my coworkers since. I don't miss any one of them, and I certainly don't want to spend any time with them, answering questions about how I'm doing, and what I'm doing in Florida without you."

"Well, what are you doing down in Florida without me?"

"You know exactly what I'm doing down there, and I want to go back." I say, splashing cold water on my face now. "But first, I'm getting out of here on my own. I can call my own cab. Please tell Carly and her young man that I had a headache and I left early." I straighten myself up, sober now from the fight, and unlock the door and stroll out of the bathroom like nothing ever happened. I'm not really sure what did just happen, but I know I feel better and I want to go home. Back to Villa Cheralena, my home.

Michael made me promise to go see Dr. Mahoney while I'm here. It seems a small price to pay for my escape, so I book an appointment for the Wednesday after Christmas.

"Tell me, what's going on with you, Teresa?"

I'm sitting on the examining table in Dr. Mahoney's office, with a green hospital gown on, tied at the opening in the back.

"I don't know," I say. "I'm having these terrible migraines and I can't sleep at night."

"That's not what I mean." She's looking into my eyes with that little flashlight. "What's going on in your life?"

"I don't know. Nothing," I say, tongue out now, in the *ahhh* position.

"You've lost a lot of weight. Are you eating at all?"

"I guess. I'm not really thinking about it."

"You? Not thinking about food?"

"I don't know. I guess I'm too busy to think about food lately. Anyway, you've always said I should drop a couple of pounds since Carly was born."

"And these headaches. When do they occur? All the time, or only at night?"

"I don't know. All the time, I guess." Suddenly I burst out crying for no reason at all. Not just a few tears, but full out sobbing like a baby.

"I'm sorry," I finally say, after my sobs subside. I wipe my red, tear-stained eyes with the tissue Dr. Mahoney has just handed me.

"I really don't know what's wrong with me," I say, "It must just be all the stress of the holidays and the renovation."

"I don't like this," she finally says, sitting down at the little table, glasses perched at the end of her nose, reading my file. She looks up. "I want you to have some tests. I'll make an appointment for you at the Cleveland Clinic in West Palm Beach, but I want you to promise me that you'll go. And try to take it easy on yourself. You're not getting any younger, you know. You can't burn the candle at both ends like you did in college, Teresa. You need rest and nourishment, for your body and your soul."

"I know, I know. Thank you, Dr. Mahoney. I guess I have been trying to do too much, with the bed and breakfast and everything. And this menopause thing isn't helping any. I can't sleep and I'm moody all the time."

"I'm going to write you a prescription for some sleeping pills. But I want you to promise me not to abuse them. That means only one a night, understand?"

"Yes, Doctor. Thank you," I say, as I get up from the table and begin to get dressed. I take the prescription, but I have no intention of taking the pills. I'm sure there isn't a pill in the world that can help me with my problem.

When I finally get home to Florida, I head straight to Villa Cheralena, only to find protestors walking up and down Flagler in front of the pier. There are about fifty of them, and they're carrying signs that read: "TEAR DOWN THE PIER" and "SAVE OUR CHILDREN." One of them even reads: "YANKEE – GO HOME." What a nightmare! I drive around the block and head for my cottage. Is that Daisy I see in the crowd?

## SEVENTEEN

Everybody has their own inner voice. That continuously running dialogue within their own head. Some have more than one. I have the old tapes of my mother, constantly criticizing me, and then I have my own tapes that I have developed over the years, that are more encouraging. The voice that I developed while raising my own daughter. And sometimes I hear another, more distant, much wiser voice. This is not a voice, really. Not in the sense that there are words spoken, but more of a feeling.

I'm walking along the beach early one morning. It's finally cool outside, but nice. The sun is just rising over the ocean. This is the place I most often hear that other, wiser voice. If there really is a God, this is where I believe he lives. Somewhere in the air between the surf and the sand, in the early, quiet hours of the morning. A sense of calm washes over me like the waves washing on shore. My hands are full of seashells. There are so many shells on the beach I could fill buckets with them, but something tells me I should only take away what I can carry. Some ancient wisdom is streaming into my consciousness faster than I can form it into words. And when I do try to form it into words, it vanishes into thin air. If I could just get quiet enough, I know I could get all the answers to my questions, but my thoughts keep fighting to stay involved in this mystic conversation. It's like I am trying to stop the very sea from rushing in and going out, rushing in and going out, like it has for all time. I finally give up trying to think at all and bend over to pick up another shell. The act of bending over to pick up shells, one at a time, like counting beads on a rosary, my simple prayer to God this morning: "Please help me. Please guide me. Please show me a sign that everything's ok."

I've been seeing things. It's Marina. She is haunting me. It started out with me catching glimpses of her, here and there, out of the corner of my eye. Sometimes I would hear a noise and when I looked to see what it was, I would catch sight of her, ducking around a corner or behind the trees. Mostly in and around the house. I know it's her. She's around eighteen years old, has long brown hair, and she is wearing that white skirt. Lately, though, this vision is getting stronger. I see her almost every night now. I think she's getting used to me. I see her in the garden, then she walks out of the gate and down the street. I know she knows I'm watching, but she doesn't seem to mind. I try to follow her, but she always disappears.

Sometimes I go to the house late at night and sit very still inside Cheralena's parlor. Suddenly I'll notice she's sitting right next to me and I get the feeling she's been there all the while. And I'm having visions of her life, of her memories. Like the dreams I've been having, only they seem more real. It scares me because I don't believe in ghosts and I think I might be going crazy. But she isn't trying to scare me. No, I think she's trying to tell me something. And sometimes I think she just wants my company. Some nights we sit in that room together, just sit there, neither one of us moving, like we're getting to know one another on some level I don't yet understand. I feel a connection to her. Sometimes I stay awake all night, just sitting there with her, and sometimes I fall asleep and dream. But these aren't my dreams I'm having. These are Marina's dreams, or rather they are her memories, her stories. Yes, I believe she is communicating to me through my dreams. I sense she wants me to help her with something, but maybe she's afraid to ask.

And when morning comes, she is gone, faded away, just as if she was a dream as well. And as the day wears on I begin to wonder if she's real or just in my imagination. I'm afraid to tell anyone for fear they'll think I'm crazy and lock me away. Maybe I am crazy. Part of me wants her to be real. She is my only real friend here, and frankly, I like her company. Telling someone else might diminish her existence. Like sharing a piece of my favorite pie, I'm afraid there won't be enough left for me.

I'm playing with that thought in my head as I pick up another shell from the sand. That small, quiet voice tells me that it is not true. There are always enough pieces of that pie. Look at all the shells on the beach. If I collected every single shell this morning and loaded them into buckets, would there be no more shells tomorrow? And isn't it true that happiness only increases when you share it? And isn't it also true that you can't keep it unless you give it away? I know that's true for love and friendship, but what about our secrets? And what about our pain and heartache? It's just the opposite, is it not? Every time we share our pain and heartache, are we not cutting it in half?

So, where does Marina stand in all of this? She is a secret right now, that is true. But if I were to tell someone about her, would she in fact start to disappear? Or would she get more real? I heard someone say once that we are only as sick as our secrets. Am I sick? Am I really going crazy down here all alone?

Just then, an older couple walks by, holding hands and laughing. The wife looks me in the eye and smiles and gives me a cheery, "Hello." I just smile and nod my head, and without a word, let them pass by. My meditation is broken by her spoken word; I am thrust out of my thoughts. I realize I'll find no more answers today, so I head back to my car to get on with my day. And as I drive back down Royal Poinciana Way, with its Royal Palm trees lining the street like solders, it occurs to me that I might never find the answers to my questions. I might never be able to help Marina with whatever she's looking for, and I might never find whatever it is that I'm looking for either.

This little adventure is not turning out to be what I thought it would be at all. I've lost my old life and my sense of self. And I'm losing my husband. We were supposed to be living out our dream retirement together. I don't even live with him anymore. I know I'm the one who pushed him away, but I didn't have to push that hard, did I? And he never really fought to stay. I thought he wanted to be involved in this with me in the beginning, but it looks like he doesn't want to leave his world just yet, or ever. I'm sure he's cheating on me, and even if he isn't, what does it matter? He's living a separate life. Away and apart from me. He's still living our old life and I'm down here living this new one all alone. I can't even remember whose idea this was in the first place, to basically get separated. To live these different lives. I also can't remember why I even loved him in the first place, and I'm not so sure I want my old life back now anyway. I really don't know what I want. I just know I want to not be crazy. I pull into the little parking lot at Villa Cheralena. The protestors are back. Why would they want to tear down the pier? What do they really care? Why does it seem like the whole world is against me?

The contractors have been spread so thin, trying to get their other projects completed before their other clients leave town. I can't wait until the season is over so we can finish this house already. The electric is complete, the mechanical is almost finished (that guy's the worst), the bathrooms are getting tiled and the kitchen is here, well the cabinets are here, in boxes anyway. I'm starting to hate the contractors. They're all idiots. They install one thing one day and tear it up the next. José says it's because I keep changing my mind. What the hell is he talking about? I'm not changing my mind. I'm just trying to get them to do it right! They actually laid the bathroom tile straight on instead of on the diagonal. Can you believe it? And when I saw it, well, naturally I had a fit.

"That's not what the drawings specify, ma'am."

"I don't care what the drawings specify. Everybody knows you lay tile on the diagonal! Especially this kind of tile, in this kind of setting!" I scream.

"Well, the drawings clearly show the tile straight on," he says.

"Tear it out!" I yell. "Tear it out or you're fired!"

I guess he told on me because I got a call from Michael.

"Teresa, honey, you can't treat these guys that way or they're going to walk out on us."

"What way? Like professionals?" All of a sudden, it's "us."

172

"You know what I mean. You have a tendency to steamroll right over people when things don't go your way."

"Go my way?" I know I'm raising my voice now, but I can't help it.

"What do you mean, go my way? Aren't I the client? Am I supposed to do things *his* way?" I shriek.

"No, honey," Michael says in his most calm, reassuring voice. You're supposed to act kind and professional. Not fly off the handle like some crazy person at every little thing."

I hate that about Michael. I know he thinks he's helping me, but all he's doing is diminishing my authority. And I think he just called me crazy.

"He's ready to walk out, Teresa. I had to talk him back. Please, please just try to be nice and let's get this thing over with, shall we?"

This thing? *This thing?* This *thing* happens to be my whole life! How dare he step in and try to take over now. What if I wanted José to walk out? I wish he would just mind his own business and leave me alone.

In the end, I had to apologize to José so he would tear up the tile and lay it properly on the diagonal. But I stopped talking to Michael, and I stopped taking his calls.

The workers are such idiots; they don't even realize I'm right there in the parlor every morning when they arrive. I suppose they will find out about this room eventually though. They are bound to realize there is another room attached to the dining room, aren't they?

The pool guy wants to get started with the renovation, but I keep putting him off. I don't want to disturb the garden.

I've been staying up nights, reading Cheralena's diary and taking long walks through the town. I can't sleep anymore. I tried taking the sleeping pills the doctor prescribed, but they don't work, so I threw them out. Instead, I've taken to having a glass of Cheralena's brandy in the evenings. Then I walk the streets of El Cid late at night. I like it when nobody's awake and I have the neighborhood all to myself. I like to pretend that I'm living back in the era when El Cid was first developed. It's easy to do. The houses haven't changed at all since then. Then I sneak back into Cheralena's parlor and find myself still there in the morning, awakened by the sound of jack hammers and wet saws. Waking up to an empty bottle and a headache. I have to sneak out the garden gate, and back to my cottage before somebody sees me. The feeling of regret is starting to tug at me, like I'm doing something wrong. I can't live this way anymore.

Tomorrow is the block party on Antique Row. I think I'll go and find that woman, Agnus. I need to talk to somebody.

The old trolley stops just north of Monroe Drive on Dixie Highway. I get out and walk south in the middle of the crowded street. The street is closed off to traffic and there are people everywhere. Mothers pushing their baby strollers, toddlers with balloons, teenagers with skateboards; the whole town is out in the streets today. There are high school marching bands and baton twirlers. Vendors are selling arepas and empanadas, and chicken with black beans and rice from the backs of their food trucks, parked on both sides of Dixie Highway. The smell of garlic and saffron fills the air. There are drink stands offering frozen piña coladas and rum runners, in colorful plastic margarita glasses, with little umbrellas in them. It feels more like Mardi Gras or Carnevale than an end-of-season sale. There are stilt walkers in colorful costumes dancing to samba music, and African dancers in full-feathered head gear, beating their drums to the music. I make my way through a sea of red and orange and purple and yellow feathers mixed with streamers and beads, and people in elaborate masks, dancing and twirling in the crowd.

Then I see her. Agnus is standing in front of her shop wearing long, silk, black and white vertical-striped bell bottoms, and a bright orange and purple flowered top with off-the-shoulder, long puffy sleeves and a ruffled neckline. She looks like one of those stilt walkers, only she can pull it off and make it look elegant. Her hair is teased out to a full Afro and she is wearing glass beads and her signature big gold hoop earrings. She holds her arms out to welcome me and embraces me in a warm hug. Was she this tall when I last met her? I look down and notice her nine-inch platforms.

"The key—what did you do with it?" she yells over the noise of the crowd.

For a split second, I don't realize what she's asking. Her question seems so urgent, I wonder if I was supposed to bring it back or give it to someone.

"I, I hung it up in the house," I yell back.

"Good, good. She'll find it," she almost whispers, and then out loud,

"Welcome, my dear. I am so glad you came." She seems genuinely pleased to see me, and I am relieved and happy to see her as well.

"Wow," I say, "What an event!" I get this feeling that this woman can help me. I'm going to take a risk and talk to her, I don't know why, but I feel that she will understand and even protect me.

"Come, my dear. Come inside." She hands me a fruity drink with rum in it as she ushers me into the tiny, air-conditioned store and closes the door.

We sit side by side on a red velvet settee, not unlike the one in Cheralena's parlor. I'm feeling a little awkward and shy, but she's acting like we had an appointment and she's been anticipating this meeting for a while. So, I sip my drink and try to relax.

"Well, have you found what the key belongs to?"

"No, I haven't," I lie. I don't know why I just lied to her, but I haven't told a soul about the secret room yet, and the question came so suddenly, I didn't know what else to say.

"What did you do with it then?"

"I hung it up in the house." I don't specify exactly where I hung the key up, but this seems to satisfy her. I'm not sure what this woman knows, but I have the feeling she knows more than I am giving her credit for. I have a feeling she knows quite a lot, and I'm about to find out. I toy with the idea of making small talk, ask her where she's from, but she gets right down to it.

"Poor Miss Cheralena, she was cursed from the start. They say the Okeechobee hurricane almost took her away, and when the wind god comes for you, you'd better go, else you'll be blowin' in the wind with no direction for the rest of your days. Yes sir, that storm was a big one, they say. Took her whole family. Almost took poor Cheralena too, except some white folk pulled her up through the attic of their house and on to the roof when the floods came. They sat there for three days waitin' on the waters to subside. It was only after they climbed down off that roof, they realized just how bad it really was. Thousands of people died in that storm, mostly pickers from Spain. Poor Miss Cheralena's parents were among the lost. Them white folk brought her to Palm Beach and left her on the steps of the church."

I just sit there and nod, wondering if she knows how much I really need this. Just to be able to talk to someone about it. I think Agnus senses my feelings and she reaches over and squeezes my hand before continuing.

"Every Easter, the church would have an Easter egg hunt for the orphans. Dress them all up pretty and invite the rich island families to come and watch. If they were so inclined, they could pick out a child just for themselves and take them home. Some were adopted, but most were just taken in as workers. The boys would become groundskeepers and the girls would become house maids.

If you were fair skinned and pretty though, like Miss Cheralena, you were lucky, you were treated like family. Well, almost like family. After all, she was still just a picker's daughter."

"But Miss Cheralena did ok. By the time I went to work for her, she was a prominent lady of El Cid. She owned that big house and had plenty of money. Only thing was, she was a widow. And she was with child. Being a pregnant widow and living all alone has its challenges. But this pregnancy was something different, something a whole lot worse."

"I was only nine years old at that time, but I delivered that baby, yes, I did. All by myself. I'll never forget that morning for as long as I live. It was the scariest thing I ever experienced. I kept thinking that old lady was going to die right there in front of me and leave me all alone to clean up the mess and tend to her newborn. There was so much blood, and she was screaming like nothing I've ever heard. You see, where I come from in St. Croix, delivering babies is no big deal. The women are tough and strong, and I seen a few deliveries in spite of my young age. But I never seen anything like this. This white woman was so frail and in so much distress, I didn't think she was going to pull through. But she did, and I guess I saved her life that day. I stopped the hemorrhaging by using an old technique the Santeria midwives taught me back in my homeland. Basically, pressing my hand on her stomach with all my might."

Wow, maybe Agnus needs to talk to someone also. Maybe she needs to tell me this story just as much as I need to hear it. This time it was I who reached over and squeezed her hand. She just looked at me and smiled.

"After that I just took care of the two of them until Miss Cheralena was well enough."

I can hear the party going on in the street just outside Agnus' little store. I feel transplanted into another time and place, it's so surreal. I can't believe I'm sitting here listening to this woman, Marina's nanny, tell this story.

"After Marina turned five years old and started school, Miss Cheralena needed the money, so she reopened the boarding house. The soldiers were coming home from war and housing was in short supply in South Florida. The government gave incentives to anyone who could provide housing to them. Marina grew up with a house full of single young men, and when she reached puberty, well they began to take notice of her. Miss Cheralena was a bit of a recluse by this time, spending all her time upstairs in that observation room looking out to sea. She either didn't notice or didn't care that those boys were bringing the local girls home with them and throwing wild parties until well into the night. I kept out of the way, mostly. My job was to cook and clean, and I needed the job, so I did what I was told. And I took care of Marina."

"You see, I was an orphan too, and I know what it's like. I had no family when I came to the States. I got myself onto a ship that was bringing cargo from the Islands. You see, I grew up with a gang of pirates and witches. I never really knew who my mother and father were, and I wanted a better life for myself. I wanted to be a true American. I had no idea how bad the South was in those days. I heard they freed the slaves, and I thought all the black people in America were rich and living the golden life just like the whites. I was so young and naïve. But when I got here, I had nothing, and no means to support myself. I considered myself lucky to have found a job cleaning and cooking for Miss Cheralena. I considered myself lucky just to have a place to live and some food to eat.

"But I loved that baby girl, yes I did. When Marina was still very young, she would stay with me. We would lay awake at night and listen to the young folk dancing to the music. It was the 1950s and everybody was drinking and partying until late into the night. I kept her out of sight mostly. As she grew older, though, she started going out and joining them. She was a wild one, that girl, but I loved her just like she was my own. But she was treated like an object by all those men at the house, and they all had their way with her, and her mother didn't seem to care. And Marina, well she just wanted to have some fun. I never had any control over her, and after all, I knew my place as a black woman in those days. I did as I was told. I did the best I could.

"Child abuse is what it really was, they handed her back and forth to each other, sometimes three different men in one night. She lived in a constant state of shame. A mere plaything to these men at night, and a miserable, confused teenager just trying to get through school during the day. Miss Cheralena spent most of her time in the observation room, drinking her homemade brandy and looking out to sea. Whenever I did try to talk to her about Marina I was told to hush up or I'd get the boot. You see, I had nowhere else to go, and I thought I could protect her somehow if I stayed on. I was only just a child myself. A child raising a child. We were doomed from the start."

"What happened to her?" I ask. But I don't think Agnus hears me. She's staring off into space, a look of anguish in her eyes. She feels guilty, I think. She didn't have a great childhood either, poor thing. She was so young and so poorly treated. What a horrific life she must have led.

Agnus stayed there in that trance for so long I thought at one point she had died. Suddenly she just started talking again without skipping a beat, as if nothing had happened.

"Then the sixties came, and we got emancipated. It was the hardest day of my life, the day I left that house. But I had to do it, you see? I just had to get out of there. I loved that little girl like my own. I would have stayed, but for the storm. But the gods were angry, you see. The gods were angry at me maybe, angry at Miss Cheralena, most likely."

"I came here to Brown Town, that's what this area off Dixie Highway was called back then. I came here and opened up this antique shop. I was the first black women to open a shop on Dixie Highway. The white folk would bring me their old furniture and I would sell it for them on consignment. That's how I made my living. It still is."

I see that faraway look in her face again. There's an odd mixture of sadness, sweetness, and regret in her eyes.

"I never should have left her, my poor baby child. I never should have let her run out of the house in the storm that night. I tell myself it's not my fault, really, how was I to know? But I should have known. When the wind god comes for you, ain't nobody can protect you."

A single tear breaks loose and rolls down Agnus' cheek. We sit there in silence for what seems an eternity. I don't want to disturb her, but then I realize she's sleeping with her eyes open.

Finally, I get up quietly and let myself out. Dusk is falling as I walk out of the shop and head north on Dixie. The party is still going strong, and I hear the celebration getting fainter and fainter in the distance, as I walk all the way back to El Cid.

I'm outraged at what Agnus has told me. Nowadays those men would all be charged with rape and Cheralena would be charged with child abuse. Poor Agnus. And poor Marina. I feel so bad for her, I want to help her even more now. If I only knew how, I would.

## EIGHTEEN

I let myself into Villa Cheralena, exhausted from the long emotional day. I slip into the parlor and flop down on the settee and close my eyes. Suddenly I hear a noise and look up. I notice the key that Agnus gave me is missing from the hook where I left it. There she is, standing in the garden, the breeze blowing through her long brown hair. I sense she is waiting for me to follow her.

*I slip out the garden gate and follow Marina down the street, past the orange house. The little orange house with the arched windows and the fountain in front. The big white house with the pair of dog statues on the pillars flanking the brick driveway. The moon is full and there's a light breeze blowing through the fronds of the coconut palms. I get to the main road and make a left, knowing just where I'm going. I cross the street when I get to the north corner of the old cemetery. I walk along the iron picket fence that surrounds the cemetery. The moonlight is playing with my shadow along the pickets like a silent flicker film at a carnival. I arrive at the gates and walk in. I am searching for something, someone. I can't seem to find them. I walk up and down the rows of headstones, looking for a name, but I can't find it. I'm sad and desperate and angry.*

Wait a minute. I've been dreaming again. That feeling of déjà vu comes over me again. I'm lying on the ground in the garden. My hands are covered in dirt and so is my white skirt. What is this? How did I get here in these clothes? What am I doing here? My head is pounding! I have to get away from this house for a while. I have to stop drinking that brandy. I'm so depressed. I'm getting too involved with these women's lives. They aren't even alive. I don't even know who I am anymore. There are no such things as ghosts. I swore to myself I wasn't going do this anymore.

I walk home to my cottage, looking over my shoulder the whole time. Is she following me? I think I see her duck behind a tree, her long white skirt visible in the moonlight. I rush inside and lock the door behind me. I go into the bathroom to wash up. What's that noise? I peek out the bathroom door and look into the living room. I think I catch a glimpse of Marina's white skirt trailing across the floor, then it's gone. There are wet footprints on the wooden floor, but they are probably just mine.

"Leave me alone!" I scream to the empty living room. "I can't help you! Go away and leave me alone!"

There she is again. I can see her clearly now, cowering in the corner of my bedroom. I think I'm scaring her by raising my voice. I start slamming doors and yelling again to scare her away, but she does not leave. She is crying now. Sitting in the corner of my bedroom, on the floor, with her knees up to her chin and her arms wrapped around her legs.

I suddenly regret yelling at her, and I say, "I'm sorry." I forget she is just a young girl, and after all she has been through, I hate to see her suffering. I sit down on the bed, still in my dirty white clothes.

"I'm so sorry, Marina," I say, calling her by her name for the first time. "Truly, I am. It's just that you're frightening me. I don't know what you want, I don't even really believe you exist. I can't help you, Marina. I'm so sorry."

Marina stops sobbing and is sitting very still with her head down on her knees and her eyes closed. I think maybe she must have fallen asleep. Do ghosts even sleep, I wonder?

I am suddenly very sleepy myself, and I lay back on my bed and close my eyes.

*It's windy and the clouds are moving slow and fast across the sky. I am flying on the wind among the clouds and I feel free for the first time in my life. All my heavy burdens are lifted. Then I remember the diary. Suddenly it starts raining very hard and I am getting wet. My skirt is getting heavy from being soaked with the rain and I am falling now. Falling out of the sky, my skirt weighing me down. I am cold and shivering. Then I hit the water and go under.*

The impact wakes me up. I have no idea how I got here, but I am lying on my stomach at the edge of the pier with my head

187

hanging over the side. I am fully awake now and I open my eyes and look into the water. I am looking at my reflection in the water by the light of the moon. But wait - that's not me. I'm looking at Marina! She is under the water looking back up at me wide-eyed. No, wait, she is dead, but her eyes are open, and they are staring right through me.

Oh my God, I'm dreaming again. I jump up, trying to jolt myself awake from this horrible nightmare, but I realize that I am already awake. This is not a dream. I really am out on the pier. I'm standing out at the edge of the pier and I am still wearing the dirty white skirt and t-shirt, and I am soaking wet. What the hell? I'm panicking now. I could have fallen in the water and drowned in my sleep. How did I get here? I bend over slightly, holding on to the piling and look into the water again to see if I can see Marina's body floating there. I see nothing at all—only blackness.

I'm shaking now from head to toe, petrified. This is the last time. I'm getting out of this place. I slowly turn around and start to walk back to my cottage. I can't sleep there tonight; I'm going to get a room at the Breakers and then I'm never coming back here. I never want to come back here. I'm alarmed and worried she'll never leave me alone. If only I can find what it is she is looking for, then maybe she'll set me free.

As I walk down the driveway to my cottage, I hear someone crying. Oh my God, it's Lucy. She is sitting on her front porch, crying softly, poor thing. I hope she didn't see me. I slip inside and peel off my dirty clothes and leave them in a pile on the floor. I step into the shower and let the warm water wash over me. I can't keep doing the same thing over and over again. I know what that means. That's the sign of insanity—I am going crazy. I get out of the shower and put on a bathrobe and a pot of coffee. There will be no more sleeping tonight. I sit at my little dining table, sipping my coffee, trying not to think, as I wait for the sun to rise.

Suddenly I am jolted by the sound of tapping on my front door. Who could that be? Tap, tap, tap.

No one comes to my door, especially not this early in the morning. Nobody even knows that I live here. I freeze, paralyzed by my fear. Tap, tap, tap.

"Teresa? Are you awake?"

Oh my God, it's Lucy. I breathe again. I get up and open the door.

"Good morning, Lucy," I say with the warmest fake smile I can muster. I must look like hell. I don't even think I combed my hair after I got out of the shower last night. She's just standing there smiling at me. I open the door wide to let her in, as I look back at the mess in my living room with her eyes. Oh my God, she must be horrified! She's my landlord, and this place looks like a bomb went off. There are dirty dishes piled up in the sink, books and papers strewn all around the house, and I can see my dirty clothes still on the floor in the bedroom. I rush over and close the bedroom door, then push the papers aside, and offer her a seat at the table.

"Coffee?" I say–too cheerily. She pretends not to notice the mess and looks right into my eyes and gives me a pitiful, motherly smile.

"No, thank you," she says as she sits down opposite me at the little dining table.

I have the feeling I've done something terribly wrong.

"I just wanted to stop by and make sure you were ok." she says. "I heard you crying last night."

Wait a minute. I thought that was her who was crying. I'm trying to wrack my brain to remember just what happened last night that she could have heard, so I don't answer right away.

"I just want you to know, whatever it is you're going through, I'm here for you. If you need me, if you want to talk about it."

I still don't answer. What could I say? That I was arguing with a ghost? I just sit there with my head down, looking into my coffee cup for an answer. We sit there in silence for an eternity, and then she reaches out and pats my hand in sympathy, much like I had done to her in the restaurant at lunch that day.

She gets up to go. I have to say something, but my mind is a grey slate. Finally, when she reaches the front door and turns to face me, all I can utter is, "Thank you." All I can feel is shame.

"Next time, come and get me, will you?" And she turns and walks out, closing the door softly behind her.

What does she mean by that? What does she know, or think she knows? Did she also see the ghost of Marina last night, or does she just think I'm some crazy drunk, talking to myself in the middle of the night? Oh my god, I wish I knew. I wish I could talk to someone. Really talk to someone. Someone who understands. Maybe I should go back and see Agnus again? But no, I don't want to upset her anymore. She's an old woman after all. I want so badly to run after Lucy and tell her the whole truth. Tell her everything from the beginning. But I can't. I can't risk it. What if she thinks I'm crazy? What if she kicks me out, or calls the police and has me Baker-acted? Or worse–calls Michael?

That afternoon, I clean up myself and the cottage and walk over and knock on Lucy's door.

"Hi, Lucy. I just wanted to come over and thank you for your kind words and compassion this morning. I guess I just had a little too much to drink last night, and I was angry with my husband. We had gotten into a terrible fight, you see, and well, I'm ok now. I just wanted to say thank you, and to tell you I'll be going away for a few days, just to clear my head. I don't want you to worry about me or anything, I assure you...."

She just stands there and looks at me patiently.

"I'm fine, really I am. Well, I'll see you in a few days then." There. I said it. Now all I have to do is get out of here for a couple of days and clear my head. The cottage is clean, so if she goes in there snooping, all looks normal. I pack a bag and head over the bridge and check into the Breakers.

Now that the season is finally over, I get a really good rate for three days. I make an appointment at the spa for a massage and a facial and I go down to the pool. I'll be fine. All I have to do is get back to the things I used to do. Eat right, go swimming, get some sunshine. I think I'll get my nails done too.

All the snowbirds are gone for the summer, back up to Canada or New York, or wherever they come from, and I have the place all to myself. I hate the tourists, and I hate the tourist season. I can't go to the market when I want. I can't even get over the bridge without waiting in a damn traffic jam during the season. But it's almost summertime now, and everything's going to be ok.

## NINETEEN

Well, the dreaded day arrives and I'm at the Cleveland Clinic for some tests my good doctor back in New York has scheduled. The clinic is disguised as an office building, situated next to an outdoor mall called City Place. The mall itself is nice enough, with a central courtyard and a fountain connected to a little a bandstand, surrounded by shops and restaurants. It's empty now because the season is over, but it's still a nice atmosphere, that is, until I walk into the clinic. I hate hospitals, and no matter how they try to disguise it, this place is definitely a hospital. I'm sitting in the waiting area just outside of radiology. Located on the 14th. floor, there's an incredible view of downtown West Palm Beach and the Island beyond. I can almost pick out my house beyond the treetops. A blind piano player in the lobby, wearing dark glasses is playing Mozart softly while his dog lies sleeping under the baby grand. One could almost be fooled into thinking it's a hotel lobby except for the signs on the doors that read; *Radiation, Blood Drop,* and *Staff Only.*

I'm not one of those people who are afraid of hospitals, I just don't like being in them because it brings up too many bad memories. I watched my mother die a slow, torturous death from cancer. She was in and out of the hospital for a year, and then finally in hospice. I hated having to take care of my mother when she was sick and dying. Not that I didn't love my mother. She was my mother, after all. Doesn't everybody love their mother? It's just that she was such a bitch, always complaining, always criticizing, but then she was pretty much like that all her life, well, all my life anyway. And being the only child, what could I do? I had to take care of her, but in the end let's just say it wasn't pretty.

My father, on the other hand, did it right. One day he wasn't feeling well and called the ambulance, the next day he was gone. That's the way I want to go. I don't want to be a burden to anybody, and I definitely don't want to make my family suffer, watching me waste away. Nope. If I had it my way, I would rather go like my father, quick and easy. Although, now that I think of it, that's how he did most things in his life. I never really saw him towards the end of his life until the funeral that is. A couple of times he tried to come back into my life. You know, the important times—when I got married to Michael, when Carly was born, the times I really didn't need him, but I guess he wanted to be included. I regretted our strained relationship at the funeral, but by then, of course, it was too late.

I'm dressed in the standard green hospital gown with the opening in the back, lying on the table as the MRI machine slowly sucks me into the tunnel. I'm trying to stay still, which is almost impossible to do when they tell you to. My mind goes back to my mother, lying there on that hospital bed, the machines hooked up to her, marking her heart rate and whatever else they do. Bags of chemo dripping into her arm. Why they didn't give her a port I'll never know, she probably refused, knowing her. I don't really remember the details all that well. She was so terrified of being put to sleep in the hospital. She refused to have the operation that could have removed the tumor that was killing her. And she wouldn't allow me to consult with the doctors without her being present. Maybe she thought I would pull the plug, I don't know. And why they were still giving her the chemo was also a mystery to me, since it was clear that it was killing her faster than the very cancer that was eating at her breast.

"Well, is it brain cancer?" I ask the technician, only half-joking.

"No, no. Nothing like that. We just want to cover all the bases. Dot our i's and cross our t's."

Why do they always say that? They just want to bilk my insurance company, that's what they really want.

"Have you been doing anything different lately? Eating anything unusual for your regular diet?" she asks.

"No," I lie. Hey, they're the ones making the big bucks, let them figure out what's wrong with me. Besides I know it's just all the dust and mold from the construction. That mixed with this menopause thing I'm going through. At least I hope that's all it is.

## TWENTY

I stayed away for three days, but yesterday I moved back into the cottage. I need to get back to work on the B & B if it's ever going to be opened on time. I decide to go back to Cheralena's parlor, to go through her things before the landscaper comes. At least that's what I tell myself. I just want to pack up the hope chest before the contractors come in here and find everything and either destroy it or steal it. I wouldn't want these treasures to be taken away from me. Tomorrow I'll go get some boxes to put everything into and put it all in storage for safe keeping. But right now, I just want to go through her things, one last time. I slip into the parlor and open the hope chest. I take out the crystal glasses, one by one, and place them on the bar. Next, I take out the silver candlesticks and hold them up to the light that's still shining in through the French doors as the sun sets in the west. They need polishing badly. I wonder if there's any silver polish behind the bar. I rummage around behind the bar and don't find any, but I do find a clean snifter and a bottle of brandy, waiting for me, calling my name. I pour myself a drink, without even thinking about it, and head over to the settee. I sit down and flip open the old photo album. The people in the photos are all strangers, yet somehow, they seem familiar to me now. I take a sip of the brandy. Just one, I say to myself. Just one glass of Cheralena's brandy for ole time's sake. As I look through the photo album, I know there's something I'm missing. Some clue maybe, as to what it is Marina is looking for. What it is she wants to tell me. I can't feel her presence in the room. Maybe she is gone, I think to myself, but I know better than that. I feel disheartened, and sorry for her. I wish I knew her when she was alive. We would have been friends, I'm sure of it.

The sun is gone now, and the moon is rising in the sky. I can't see it, but I can feel it. I try to summon up Marina. What did she look like? Did I actually get a look at her face? Was she really in my cottage or was I imagining it? I lay down on the settee and close my eyes. I fall asleep and dream:

*It's a warm autumn night and I'm out on the golf course with some boys from school. We're playing a drinking game and Joey is there and he's looking at me and smiling. Joey, the cutest boy at school and he's smiling at me. I'm on top of the world. I feel especially pretty tonight and I'm glad those mean girls aren't here. I am not one of the pretty girls and I know I'm not popular, but tonight is different. I have on my new white skirt and white lace midriff top and my hair in in long braids. We're sitting in a circle, Joey, Stevie, that older boy Billy who I don't really like, and some other boy I don't know. They're passing the bottle around and taking turns drinking while the other boys count to see how long they can chug the whiskey. Now it's my turn. I put the bottle up to my lips and throw my head back as the boys count 1,2,3… the hot liquid is burning my throat as it goes down, but I'm determined to win this game. The boys are all laughing and smiling at me. All except for Billy, who has a weird look on his face. Just then he gets up and takes the bottle out of my hands and announces; "The Winner!" as the other boys start to cheer and hoot. I'm a little confused because I thought he was mad at me or something, the way he's looking at me with that twisted smile and those burning eyes. He scoops me up just like they do in the movies when the groom carries the bride over the threshold and he starts walking, carrying me as the other boys follow like we're in a parade. I'm feeling very dizzy now so I'm happy when he lays me down on top a pile of cool, damp leaves. I'm trying to sit up now, hoping I don't get sick and throw up in front of Joey who is looking at me now with that same twisted smile. I keep trying to get up and Billy keeps pushing me back down onto the pile of leaves.*

*Then all of a sudden, he tells Billy and Stevie to hold my hands up over my head. They each have a hand and are kneeling on the ground on either side of me, laughing, when Billy gets on top of me and starts to pull my shirt off. The other boy tries to hold my legs down, but I am kicking now and saying,*

*"Stop, stop it. No, stop it!" Now Billy pulls my skirt right up to my stomach. I am screaming now and struggling to get my hands free. I am too strong for the one boy to hold my legs, and I am kicking wildly, but Billy is on top of me and pulling down my underpants. I feel flushed in my face and I am crying. Humiliated by what is happening to me and especially because Joey is a part of it. I can tell he doesn't really want to be there anymore, that he thinks it has gone too far, because Billy yells at him, "Hold her down!" I realize I am*

*about to get raped by this bully and in front of these other boys and I am filled with shame and horror. I have to get them to stop somehow and then I get an idea and I shout out, "I have my period!" even though I really don't.*

*I knew this would stop them, because at this age I already know that boys are afraid and disgusted by this function of a woman's body, and for some reason this shames me even more. Suddenly Billy gets up off of me and the other boys let go of my arms and legs and they all run away laughing, leaving me there half dressed in the middle of the golf course, on top of a big pile of leaves, crying and sobbing. I'm feeling ashamed and dirty. A mixture of hatred and shame comes over me. I hate Billy for what he just did, and I hate those other boys, but mostly I hate myself. I am ashamed and embarrassed by the whole thing. I just want to run and hide. I will never tell a soul what just happened. I vow to hate those boys forever, and to never tell a soul. As I run home, I am pushing it down, deep inside of me, where no one will ever find it. All those bad feelings get rolled into one big feeling of not being good enough, not being loved. I am dirty and there are leaves in my underpants and leaves in my hair. I feel ashamed and guilty. I am lower than scum. I want to die.*

The next thing I know, I'm awake and out on the pier again, looking into the water at my own reflection, crying, and thinking about the nightmare I just had. It seems so real to me. I'm so confused. I'm racking my brain to remember how I got out here. I'm really scared this time. I need to get off this pier. I can't believe this is even happening to me. I slowly get up, a little dizzy now, careful not to trip and fall into the water. I walk off the pier. I need help.

I walk home to my cottage and take a hot shower and wash the skirt and hang it back up in my closet. Just a few hours' sleep is all I need. Please, God, don't let me dream again tonight.

The next morning, I wake up with that feeling of dread again. Like something is hanging over me and I can't explain it. I swore I would never drink from that bottle of brandy again and that I would never put that skirt on again. I don't know why I keep doing the same things over and over again. I need to stop this.

This is the last time. I'm not ever going back there. I'm going to finish Villa Cheralena and we're going to sell it. I'm going to tell the pool guy and the landscape designer that they can start on the backyard. I'm going to tell the contractor about this room and, and what? Have it demolished? I can't do that! Maybe I'll just nail it shut and walk away. That's it. I'll just close it up and hide the past, just like Cheralena did all those years ago. I'll just close it up and walk away.

Tomorrow I'm really going to get out of this town for a while. I think I'll fly home to New York or maybe go to Boston to visit Carly. Yes, that's what I'll do. I'll go pop in on Carly. I miss her so much. I miss my family. Why did I seclude myself here all alone?

I want my old life back. I want to forget all about this place and go back to my old self again. I want to forget about Marina, and her life, and her death. I wish it never happened. I wish I never found that room, that secret room of my dreams. And I wish I never opened up that diary. I'm so depressed I want to die!

I pack my bags, all of them this time, and carry them out to the Mini. It has started to rain, and the wind is howling. I'm getting soaked as I try to stuff my suitcases into the car. After much struggle, I finally get the back door of the car closed and jump into the driver's seat, just as a bolt of lightning hits the ground right in front of me, followed immediately by a loud clang of thunder. That was close. It's pouring rain now, so heavy that I can hardly see in front of me, as I slowly pull the car out of the driveway and head south onto Dixie Highway toward Belvedere Road. The olive tree branches are whipping around so violently I think they might snap free any minute and come crashing down on my little car. The rain turns to hail and is pounding so heavily on my convertible top that I think it's going to rip right through it. I turn right on Belvedere. The noise from the hail and the wind is deafening. There isn't a soul out on the street. I realize that I don't even know what day of the week it is. I look at my phone and it's 6:00 a.m. The airport is only five minutes away, just stay calm, I tell myself, as I drive like a madwoman, all alone on the streets, the wind whipping garbage can covers around like frisbees down the street in front of me. The traffic lights are out as I get to the intersection of Australian Avenue and Belvedere Road. No matter, there are no cars on the road anyway. I turn into the airport entrance and go up the ramp to the parking garage. The arm is up, so I drive straight through. I park my car, shaking from panic now, and I get my bags and run into the airport, as if it's me the storm is chasing.

I try to compose myself as best I can before I walk up to the Jet Blue ticket counter. I can't remember the last time I actually bought a ticket at the counter of the airport, and I'm wondering how strange I must sound when I ask the attendant behind the counter if I could please purchase a one-way ticket to Logan Airport in Boston.

He laughs out loud as if I'm joking, and says, "Lady, there are no flights coming in or going out while this storm is upon us."

I almost ask him what storm but thank him instead and turn around and walk over to the newsstand at the end of the terminal. There are several TVs on, all set to the Weather Channel. Oh my God, we're having a hurricane! I realize I haven't even looked at the news—or the weather for that matter—in weeks now. We could be in the middle of World War III, and I wouldn't even know it!

There's a guy standing behind the counter and I ask in my most casual voice, "Is it headed right for us?"

"Oh, no. It's gonna turn north by midnight. But we'll feel the brunt of these feeder bands for the next couple of days or so. That's if we're lucky. If it doesn't stall off the coast and soak us till the fall."

Defeated. Utterly worn down and defeated, I turn and get myself out of the airport as quickly as my feeble legs can carry me. I need to get out of here before anybody sees me cry. I get to the car, put my luggage back in, sit myself back in the driver's seat, and totally break down. Crying all the way home, I don't know which is blinding me more, the rain pounding on my windshield or my own tears.

"Ok, I surrender! I give up!" I scream into the wind.

I don't know what to do. I get myself back to the cottage and stay there for the duration of the storm. Eating nothing by peanut butter and saltines and drinking nothing but water. I simply wait it out for three days. Day and night the rain comes down and the wind howls, as if the very heavens are crying, one feeder band after the next; the storm has indeed stalled off the coast. There are trees down everywhere. José texted me just before the power went out to tell me not to worry—Villa Cheralena is safely boarded up, ready to ride out the storm.

"Great—thanks. Just what I needed to hear," I think to myself.

I pace the floors of my little cottage day after day. Alternating from crying to sleeping, and then to crying again, until finally I'm numb. No more fury—just resignation. Then as if I were the very cause of the storm, the wind calms down with me, and the rain lets up as my tears begin to dry.

## TWENTY-ONE

It's been nine months since we bought Villa Cheralena. I'm in the sitting room on the third floor, watching the sunrise over the water. It finally stopped raining. Boy, when it rains down here, it really rains. For so many days now, I can't count them. Pouring rain, like a deluge of water just dropping out of the sky. I thought it would never stop. The streets are flooded and the ground is saturated. And when it finally stopped, I could see the steam coming up from the street, it's so hot.

I've tried to stay away, but I can't. I need to see Marina. I miss her and I want to help her. And I want her to help me too. Only if I could help her find what she's looking for. Then maybe she will be free. And then maybe so will I.

The construction has been delayed due to the storm. The pool guy never started. Turns out he was a fugitive from the law and got arrested and thrown in jail for something or other. I never did call another pool contractor.

Michael's coming tomorrow. He booked a room at the Breakers. Seems he wants to come check on his investment, but not his wife. I didn't answer the phone when he called because I didn't feel like fighting. All we ever do is argue lately. I suppose I'll have to face him sooner or later. We're meeting at the house tomorrow at noon. He wants to walk the property and do a punch list. It seems we're behind schedule. I don't care. I haven't told him about the parlor or Marina, and I don't want to. I'm hoping he gets fed up and goes away and leaves us alone. I'm not ready to share my secret just yet. I might never be.

I'm at the house when Michael arrives in his shiny BMW rental. Even though it's too hot to put the top down, I notice he sprung for the convertible. He gets out of the car dressed in a light grey suit. I'm wearing a long white cotton skirt and T-shirt with flip flops, and my hair is up in a high ponytail.

We great each other like we're strangers. It's been so long; I can't even remember the last time we made love.

"You look different," he says, in a sad but somewhat sarcastic way.

"So do you," I say, although I'm sure he's not the one who's changed.

"I made some calls and found another pool contractor," he says.

"Great," is all I can think to say to this.

"Teresa, what's the matter with you?" I can tell he's angry with me already, and I get defensive.

"What? Nothing," I say.

"Look at you! I come all the way down here to see you, and you're dressed like that?"

"How am I supposed to dress? It's the dead of summer and I'm living on a goddamn construction site!" I scream. "Was I supposed to get my hair and nails done, and have a suit on?" I say, gesturing to him, who in my opinion is the one who looks out of place here.

"You don't even have any makeup on. And what have you done to your hair?" he says.

Sorry I don't look up to par, buddy, but I'm fighting for my life here, is what I want to say, but what comes out is, "Oh, go to hell."

"Listen, I'm trying to be reasonable here," he says.

"No, you're not. You're trying to argue with me."

"Teresa, tell me, what is it? You have to tell me, what's going on here?" He takes me by the shoulders. We're standing in the middle of the great room. Outside the sun is shining, and the crystals on the chandeliers are throwing rainbows all around the shiny black and white marble floor. The room looks exactly as he first drew it all those months ago. It's so surreal, for an instant I feel like taking him in my arms and dancing, like we're in some romantic dream. For a split-second I even see that old familiar look in his eyes. The one I used to love.

But this isn't a romantic dream. This is cold, hard reality. The look in his eyes is faded now, replaced with impatience and frustration. He's gone, my husband, the love of my life—he's gone. A stranger to me now.

"Teresa!" He still has me by the shoulders, and he's shaking me now. Is it anger or panic I see there?

"Let me go," I say, and I pull free of his grip and turn toward the grand stair. So beautiful, so elegant. I've really restored this room to its original glory. I can almost hear a Chopin waltz playing softly in the background. The baby grand will go right over there.

"Teresa!" he snaps, impatiently.

"Michael, I don't know what you want from me. I'm doing the best I can. I don't know why you came all the way down here just to call a pool contractor. You could have done that from New York."

"I came to see my wife," he says, sadly. "But I can see that she's not here."

And with that, he turns and walks out the front door, slamming it behind him.

I stand still, in the middle of the great room, the music pauses, I wait, holding my breath. Then I hear him start up the car and pull out of the parking lot.

"Michael! Wait!" I go running out the front door and down the walk. "Please don't go! I need you!" But it's too late. He's gone. Roaring down Valencia Drive, rubber tires burning, never looking back.

For three days now, I've been like this. Sitting like a zombie in the observation room, looking out to sea, phone in hand, waiting for him to call. Wondering if I should call him, just to say "Hi, I'm sorry," but I never use the phone. Every night I walk the streets of El Cid. Up and down the lake blocks, back and forth on the wall at Flagler. Just walking, not thinking, not crying either. Numb, waiting, pacing.

What should I do? What do I want to do? What can I do? Can I live without him? Do I want to? I wonder how our relationship got like this. Why is it he's the parent and I'm the child all of a sudden? And why do I dread being all alone? It's not the actual being alone that I dread so much as not belonging to somebody. I actually like being alone. I thought I had it just perfect. Him out of town and me living another, separate life away from him. But this life is not real, and I know that. But what do I owe him?

I walk back to the cottage to shower and wait for the sun to come up and signal another empty day with no human contact and no end in sight.

I want my life back, but I'm not sure I want the life I used to live anymore.

## TWENTY-TWO

I'm in the parlor, sitting on the settee one warm summer night, sipping some brandy. I look up and notice the key is missing from its hook again. This tells me Marina is around somewhere. She's accustomed to coming in and taking it off the hook for some reason. Maybe she wants me to go walking with her. I look outside and see her in the garden, the light of the full moon glowing all around her. She has her back to me, and she is on her hands and knees in the corner of the garden. The marble plaque with her name on it is laying off to one side, and she is digging in the ground where it sat.

I walk outside, my brandy in hand. She turns and sees me standing there. She pulls a box out of the hole she had just dug and holds it up to me. What is this? I walk over and sit down, cross-legged on the grass in the moonlight. She hands me a steel cash box and I open it to find a plastic bag inside, filled with papers. They are the missing pages from Cheralena's diary. There are also letters, tied up with a red satin ribbon, some newspaper clippings, and a photo.

I skim the newspaper clippings first. They are all about the war and the sightings of German U-boats patrolling off the coast of Florida. There is one about how the local yachtsmen and fishermen would go out in their private vessels to guard the coastline and report to the Navy on any U-boats they spotted in the night.

There is another article about an Italian sailor being captured just off the coast of Palm Beach. The article tells of how the enemy sailors would sneak on shore at night, by the light of the moon, and steal food and supplies from the local markets. Some would even spend the night in the local brothels. There was a mention of a particular brothel in El Cid.

Next, I read the missing pages from the diary. They are worn and stained, and I take my time, and read every word slowly:

"It was he. It was he who killed my husband. My lover, the love of my life. He killed my husband."

Geo and his crew were rowing back to sea to meet the submarine one night after spending the evening at Villa Cheralena. It was a full moon and Johnny Cotton and his men could easily spot the little inflatable boat in the water, although they had been drinking quite a lot that evening. The other men just wanted to scare them, have some fun with them, but Johnny was out for revenge. He had heard that the tall one, the leader, was sleeping with Cheralena, and Johnny wanted him to pay. So, when they came upon the little boat in Johnny's 60-foot sport fisherman, and the guys were yelling and firing shots into the air over the heads of the sailors; that's when Johnny stood up, pulled the pin on the hand grenade he was holding, and threw it right at the leader, yelling;

"That will teach you to fuck another man's wife, you bastard"

Geo knew exactly what was coming, and who was attacking him and why. The moonlight was so bright, and the fishing boat was so close, he could see the expressions on the other men's faces. He watched them change from disbelief, to shock, to horror, first as Johnny Cotton threw the hand grenade, then as he grabbed his oar, stood up, and just like they did in their favorite American pastime, Geo swung his hardest and hit that grenade right back at Johnny Cotton. It would have been a home run had it been an actual ballgame, but instead it blew Johnny Cotton right out of the boat. The other men, seeing what was coming, jumped overboard to save themselves and watched helplessly as their friend got blown to pieces and then his boat sank.

They all made it back to shore, that is all but Johnny Cotton, although his body parts were already washing ashore the next day as his buddies re-told the story of what had happened.

The young Italian sailors never went back to Villa Cheralena the next day or the days after that. Eventually, though, Geo did go back to Cheralena and was captured upon his return. Someone spotted him and called the authorities. They found him foolishly trying to sneak away by the little marina in front of Villa Cheralena and they arrested him and shipped him off to prisoner of war camp.

I read on;

"Why did he tell me this? Does he think I could forgive him? I never can. He stole my future away from me. He took all that I had worked so hard to accomplish and destroyed it. I haven't told him the news yet, that I am carrying his child. He is the enemy after all. What can I do? I can't just pretend that it's alright. It's not alright. Yes, I am in love with the enemy. The murderer who killed my husband is my lover. But we cannot possibly go on like this, knowing what happened; I know there is no future with him. I must send him away and lock up this secret until the day I die. Our unborn child must never know about him and he must never know about our child."

Afterward, Cheralena closed down the boarding house and kept to herself. The townspeople suspected she was running a brothel anyway and were glad when the business shut down.

Marina hands me my glass of brandy. I take a sip and read on.

"I am pregnant. Yes, there is a tiny little life growing inside me and I can feel it. I dream about him and his unborn child every night. When I awake, I think it was all just a dream, but then I feel it. The stirring inside me, like little butterflies in my stomach. Soon those butterflies turn to nausea and I have to go throw up. I am violently ill every morning and stay in bed until noon. I can no longer care for myself and this house, so I have decided to close down the boarding house. I have informed all my tenants that they must relocate by the end of the month."

"They are calling us whores. I am not a whore! Maybe those other girls are whores, but I am not. I was so naïve. Why did I ever take him in? Why did I have to fall in love with the enemy? Agnus, my colored girl, will stay on. Agnus is the only one who knows the truth, I suspect, but she will never tell. She has no family of her own and she doesn't want me to kick her out in the streets. Besides, I think she's looking forward to raising the baby. I am not. I want to kill myself. "

Pages and pages of Cheralena's heartache, all neatly folded and buried for so many years. These are the pages Cheralena had torn out of her diary so no one could see. She must have been hiding them from Marina, and Marina must have found them and read them, and then buried them again, so no one would ever know the truth. Only me. But why only me? What do I have to do with them? And why is she showing them to me now? I read on:

"What have I done? He's sending me letters from prison. He says he's forgiven me, but I have not forgiven him, and I cannot forgive myself—ever. I went from a respectable young bride, to a widow, to a whore all in one short spring. I was going to be part of society, and now I cannot even leave the house for the shame of it all. Any my unborn child will have to grow up with this shadow hanging over its sad, sorry life."

Soon afterward, the child was born. She named her Marina. Cheralena claimed she was the daughter of her deceased husband who had died so heroically in the war. But the townspeople suspected the truth. It was all over the papers, the day the Italian sailors were captured off the coast and sent to prison in Jacksonville. And she kept all the clippings.

Marina sits quietly next to me in the garden, crying softly in the moonlight. I want to reach out to her, but I don't dare for fear she might disappear. I take another sip of brandy. Next, I read the letters. They are all from him, Cheralena's lover. They are all in order. I read the first one....

February 22, 1940

My Dearest Cheralena,

You are my only soul. My life and my every breath. The last time we held each other will be forever in my memory. When I went back to the docks that last night, they were waiting for me. The rest of my crew had already been captured and they shipped us off to prison somewhere upstate. I hear rumors they are sending us to a war camp in Nebraska. By the time you get this letter, I will probably already be gone.

I will come back for you, my love.

The handwriting looks so familiar. I look up at Marina.

"Who is it?" Do I know him?"

She just looks at me, tears softly rolling down her cheeks.

I gently fold the letter and take out another.

March 15, 1940

My love,

I cannot expect you to wait for me, as I am in prison. But I am not the enemy, only a victim like you are, my love. And I promise you, my darling, I will get back to you somehow. Just as soon as this crazy war is over, I will be back. Then we can pick up where we left off, and we can be together again, forever.

You are my soul, my life, my only breath.

I wonder why he never came back.

I fold that letter and place it back on the pile and read another.

April 4, 1950

My Dearest Darling,

Why won't you see me? I will not go away until you see me.

I saw our love child. I know she is my daughter. She looks just like me. What did you name her? Is she happy? Please let me back in your life. The war is over, my love. I realize much time has gone by, but eternity is not too long to wait for you. We can pick up where we left off and live our dream together. Please, if only for the sake of our beautiful daughter. Please let me come back into your life.

You are my soul, my life, my only breath.

And another.

May 7, 1950

Dearest Darling,

I came again today. I saw you working in the garden and then you went inside. I know you saw me. Please, my love. Please let me in. I will not leave you alone until we speak. I have a good job now, if that's what you're worried about. I'm an architect. I can support you and our beautiful daughter. What is her name?

## TWENTY-THREE

He was an architect? Marina's biological father was an architect? My head is spinning. Wait a minute—

Marina's father was an Italian sailor during the war. He must have been twenty years old when he got captured. And he came back here years later, to try and rekindle his relationship with Cheralena, in Florida, the place he loved most.

I'm immobile for a good ten minutes, in shock and disbelief. I don't want to know what I think I'm learning. I look at the last letter in the pile. I look at Marina, she just nods. I carefully pick it up and read.

June 30, 1950

My dearest darling Marina,

I am writing this letter against the wishes of your mother. You see, I am your real father, and your mother has kept this secret from you to protect you, my love, but I can no longer keep silent. I love your mother very much and I believe she still loves me.

We were very young when we first met, no older than you are now. There was a war going on, and I was the enemy, you see.

But we fell in love anyway. I am not the enemy now, my dearest child.

I have come back to be with you, and I have tried to reason with her, but your mother can be a very stubborn woman.

So, I am going away, but I want you to know that you are loved. I will always love you and your mother, and I will hold you both in my heart forever.

Love,

Of course, Geo is the American version of Giovanni.

I read the last line. He signed his name this time:

Your Father,

Giovanni Dontelli

I look up at Marina, still sitting in the moonlight. She is looking straight at me with tears in her eyes, and I know by the look on her face that she must have known all along. She must have recognized me. Marina's father wasn't just any Italian sailor who got caught sneaking ashore during the war. He was my father!

The moon comes out from behind a cloud and lights up the garden. I look at Marina as if for the first time and recognize the family resemblance. She is my sister! My half-sister. I didn't want to believe it at first, but there is no denying it. No wonder I know her so well. No wonder I can see her when no one else can. And this house! I have been dreaming of this house for years. And the dreams! That's why the dreams are so real. We were, still are, connected on some cellular level, she and I.

I think back to the stories my mother used to tell me about my father when he was a sailor in the Italian navy, and how he got captured off the coast of Florida in the 40s. She would tell me the crew would sneak ashore to go to a brothel, but I never knew he was in love with another woman before my mother. But there is no denying it.

Just then, Marina hands me the photo. There he is, my father, standing with Cheralena in the garden. He was very young. I am crying now and so is Marina.

I suddenly realize what she has been looking for in the graveyard all these years. I take her by the hand and together we walk out of the garden gate and down the street, past the little orange house with the arched windows and the fountain in front. Past the big white house with the pair of dog statues on the pillars flanking the brick driveway.

I love this street. We cross the street when we get to the north corner of the old cemetery. We walk along the iron picket fence that surrounds the cemetery. There are two shadows flickering in the moonlight along that picket fence tonight. We arrive at the entrance gates and walk in.

I lead Marina to the grave of my father. Yes, of course, this is the cemetery where my father was laid to rest. This is where he wanted to be buried all those years ago. This is where those volunteer veterans played "Taps" for him at his funeral. I thought it strange at the time, but his last will and testament specified this very cemetery, and the plot was even pre-purchased before he died.

Marina couldn't find it because her ghost was still only a twenty-two-year-old girl. My father died years after Marina did. She was stuck in the past and couldn't see any of the new headstones. She needed me to bridge the gap, somehow, and I did exactly that.

I show her the grave of our father and we kneel down, side by side, and we both pray. We say a prayer for him, and we say a prayer for each other. We pray for forgiveness, and we pray to forgive.

Marina's father loved her all her life, but she never got to know that. It's not enough to just love someone, but you must show them that love in a way they can understand it. And with our children, we must show that love while they're still young. I understand now that it's also not enough to just love someone, but that love must be given away, it must be shared for it to do any good in this life.

Finally, we get up and walk back to the house.

"We must burn these letters and finally let the past go. Help me get rid of this stuff and you will finally be free, my sister," I whisper.

We walk back through the open garden gate and into the house, into Cheralena's parlor, the two of us.

I pile the diary, the letters, and the newspaper clippings on top of the wooden chest, with the photograph of our father and Marina's mother on top. Then I pour the last of the homemade brandy onto the pile. We kneel down together, side by side once again. Then I light the match. Up it goes, flames shooting to the ceiling, as we both say goodbye to the past. I am crying and she is crying. Tears of release—cleansing tears.

We have so much in common after all, my half-sister and me. I think about all the dreams—Marina's memories. I hope this will help heal her of all those sad, awful memories she has been keeping locked up inside. And then I think about all my own sad, awful memories of growing up without a father. All the hurt I have locked up inside myself. Maybe it is Marina who came back to heal me. The flames are high and hot now. I hear glasses breaking at the bar. I smell the stuffing from the settee burning. Then blackness washes over me.

## TWENTY-FOUR

It is 2:00 am when Michael gets the call. There has been another fire at the house. This time Teresa is hurt. And this time, it looks like she started it. She is in the ICU at Good Samaritan Hospital with third-degree burns. Michael thanks the officer and hangs up. There is nothing he can do but wait until morning. He feels so helpless. He books the first flight out, and gets showered and dressed, and heads out to LaGuardia Airport. He arrives at the airport at 3:30 a.m. for a 6:00 a.m. flight.

There is always someplace open in the airport in New York, and he finds a coffee bar and manages to get a muffin and some coffee into his system. He then proceeds to walk the terminal by his gate. He walks up and down the blue carpet tile, all alone except for the cleaning crew and a couple of other airport workers at this hour.

"Why would she want to burn the house down and kill herself in the process?" Did Michael have any indication that she was having suicidal thoughts? He had answered no to that question when the hospital called, but he can't help but wonder. He feels as empty as the terminal he is pacing. A void has opened up in his very soul. Why did Teresa want to kill herself? He blames himself, of course. He should have never left her alone down there for so long. He knew he was losing her. She had changed so dramatically the last time he saw her, but he was so busy, and too wrapped up in his own work to notice at the time. So he chose to ignore what he now knows were the warning signs. The changes in her appearance, in her attitude towards him. The glaring red flags, trying to tell him that his wife was turning into something he did not even recognize anymore. Choosing instead to feel annoyed by her, and impatient with the whole situation down there.

He was actually thinking of telling her that he wanted to call the whole thing off. This whole thing had gone on too long already. He had decided it wasn't such a good idea after all, this bed and breakfast thing. He had intended to put his foot down and tell Teresa that he was taking over the construction and selling the place upon its completion. He was going to insist that she come back home with him and let this whole idea go, or he wanted a divorce. But he didn't want a divorce. No, he doesn't want a divorce. No, he wants his wife back. He wants the Teresa he used to know and love back. He only hoped it wasn't too late now. Too bad the entire house didn't burn down. He is sick of that house. He never wants to set foot in there again.

It seems there was an additional room just off the dining room that he didn't know about. That was the only room that burned down. Burned right down to the ground. With nothing left but the dirt below, and the sky above. And then the fire was contained. Teresa was found lying in the garden just outside the burned-out room. It looked like someone had dragged her unconscious body out of the burning house and laid her among the ivy and the bougainvillea.

Teresa is asleep in a private room in the ICU when Michael arrives at the hospital at last. She is hooked up to machines that are humming and beeping, showing her heartbeat and other vital signs. There are tubes coming out of her arms that are attached to bags of fluid hanging by her bedside, and another tube of oxygen is wrapped around her face. She looks like death itself, and Michael doesn't know if he can stand to be in the room with her. She still has the smell of burnt flesh about her.

He slips out into the hallway and breaks down in tears. Someone comes by and ushers him into a small private office.

"Mr. Peters? I'm Dr. Anderson. Your wife is going to be ok, but she has been through a lot."

Michael wipes his eyes with the back of his hand and just nods his head and looks into his lap.

"We are going to keep her in the ICU for another day or two and then move her to a room in progressive care as soon as her vitals are stable. The burns will take some time to heal."

"How long?" is all Michael can think to say.

"Weeks, maybe months, but she will heal. She will have some scarring, but she will heal."

Michael nods his head again and continues looking at his hands, now folded in his lap.

"There is something else." Dr. Anderson shifts his position in his chair, as if he doesn't quite know how to say what he is going to say next.

Michael catches sight of the doctor's body language and sits up straight in his chair. He's looking the doctor straight in the eyes for the first time, as he braces himself for the worst.

"What?" He feels out of control, helpless in front of this man. And whenever Michael feels helpless, his emotions turn to quiet anger.

"We want your permission to run some tests. We're not sure, but we suspect your wife has a form of dementia called LBD."

Michael has no idea what the doctor just said. It is as if he is listening to a foreigner speak another language, but he knows it isn't good by the look on the doctor's face. He has the sensation of falling.

"What is LBD exactly?" he finally asks, against his own will. He didn't want to ask that question, and he certainly doesn't want to hear the answer.

Michael had been skydiving once in his life. He remembers being coaxed out of the plane with his parachute on his back and the cord in his hand. He didn't like the feeling at all. Waiting to pull that cord, counting down the fifteen seconds. It was the longest torture of his life. And when he finally did pull the cord and he felt the parachute jerk him up and he knew he was in control again; he swore to himself that he would never do that again. Sitting here in this office, waiting in the eternity of silence for this strange doctor to deliver Teresa's death sentence and Michael's fate, he feels just as he did back then. Like he's free falling. He even starts counting backward from fifteen. Only this time there is no cord. He's certain he's going to smash into the ground any second now.

"Dementia with Lewy Bodies is a type of progressive dementia. We think it is caused by microscopic calcium deposits on the brain. Eventually these abnormal deposits will lead to a decline in thinking and reasoning. The patient will experience recurrent visual hallucinations or delusions, such as seeing shapes or colors in the air around them. Sometimes they see people or animals that aren't there, or they start talking to deceased loved ones. Eventually there is a mental decline. The inability to plan. Extreme swings between alertness and confusion, sleep disturbances...."

Michael has to stop listening and is counting backwards again in his head. He cannot and will not listen to this man, this stranger, telling him these horrible things about his wife. What does he mean, "the patient?" She is not just a "patient" lying there covered in third-degree burns. This is his wife he is talking about. She has a name, dammit!

"Including insomnia or acting out dreams," the doctor continues.

"No, no! Not Teresa!" The scream is coming from inside his head.

"No known treatment or cure," Dr. Anderson goes on to say.

What has happened to his lovely, lively, beautiful wife? How did he let it go this far? Why did he let it get so out of hand? There must be some mistake. Who does this guy think he's talking to? This is not our doctor. This is just some stranger that doesn't know anything about us. Doesn't know anything about Teresa. Doesn't know how smart and funny she is. Or how we struggled so hard to have a child when we were young, and how strong she was during those early baby days. Or what a good mother she was, and still is. Or what a great wife and partner she is.

"We can't be certain, even after the results from the tests come back, but there are certain markers."

Again, all Greek. The doctor is speaking Greek.

"She has been hallucinating. In fact, she is having severe hallucinations."

"What?" Suddenly, Michael is pulled back to earth and the doctor is speaking English again. "You mean she is seeing things? Like she is crazy?"

"No, we don't think she is psychotic, and she is not showing the typical signs of schizophrenia, so, no, not crazy in that sense. But she claims she has been communicating with a relative who has passed. And she says she is having very vivid dreams about this person. All signs of LBD."

"You mean she's seeing ghosts?"

"Well, yes, you could say that. At least she thinks she is seeing a ghost, but that's all part of her condition. That is, we suspect that it is."

"I'd like to get another opinion." This guy is the one who's crazy!

"Of course, but—"

Michael stands up and abruptly cuts off Dr. Anderson. He doesn't want to hear any more. Feeling strong now in his anger and wanting to protect his wife from this crackpot, he turns and walks right out of the room. There must be a specialist in this area.

Michael continues to walk right out of the hospital without another word. He heads over the bridge to the Breakers and checks into a room. He orders a double scotch on the rocks from room service, and proceeds to make some phone calls. He finds a private psychiatric hospital on the island. Teresa will be moved there in a couple of weeks, as soon as her burns heal.

"Hey, how are you feeling?" Michael stands at the foot of Teresa's bed at the Seaside Hospital for Mental Health. This is his first visit with her since he had her moved here from the hospital after her burns healed. It is a quaint little facility, tucked away between the tall shade trees and the ocean on the north end of Palm Beach. Guarded by lush tropical foliage and an imposing front gate, it looks like any other mansion on the island. He liked the look of the place as much as he hated the name. The doctors are discrete and professional, and it is costing him a fortune to have her here, but he has hope that Teresa will fully recover.

"Hi, Michael. It was Marina. I met the ghost of my half-sister, and her name was Marina. That's who saved me, you know. She pulled me out of the burning house."

He doesn't know how to respond to this, so he just nods and smiles. She looks so much better today. Her scars are healing nicely, and she looks serene and almost happy.

"Is there anything you need? Anything I can get you?" he asks.

"No, thank you, Michael. And don't look so worried. I'm going to be all right. How's the house coming?"

"Let's not talk about that now. I can only stay for a few minutes, but I'll be back later this afternoon. I have to go down to the office and take care of the paperwork. I just wanted to make sure you were all right."

"I'm fine, honey. You go. I'll be here when you get back."

And with that, Michael slowly turns and walks out of the room and down the lushly carpeted hallway to the elevators at the end of the hall. They gave Teresa a corner room with a view of the ocean. She'll like that. Just like the Breakers. Michael is determined to do whatever it takes to get his wife back. He realizes just how much he needs her, now that he almost lost her.

## TWENTY-FIVE

"Hello, Teresa, my name is Dr. Susan Wilson, and I'm going to help you get well again."

"Hello," I say, without acknowledging the fact that I don't believe her. She's the third doctor I've seen so far, and the other two just told me I have an incurable disease.

I'm sitting on a white chintz sofa facing an enormous picture window in a room right out of Southern Homes magazine. Dr. Wilson is sitting in one of the two high-back armchairs facing me, with her back to the picture window, and the glorious view of the ocean behind her. Between us sits a whitewashed coffee table, piled high with books and shells, and beneath our feet lies a sisal rug. Dr. Wilson's desk, whitewashed to match the coffee table, sits in the corner of the room facing out toward the beautiful view. The walls are lined with books and nautical décor, and the room is sunny and cheerful.

"You may call me Susan, and I hope you don't mind if I call you Teresa?"

"Not at all."

"I believe we are going to be good friends before this is over, and I want you to know you can trust me. Whatever we discuss here will be in the strictest confidence. That means that I won't ever tell your husband or any of your other doctors what you say—no matter what. Okay?"

"Okay'" I say.

"Dr. Jones and Dr. Radcliff think you have a disease called Lewy Bodies Dementia. Do you know what that is?"

"Only what they just told me," I say. I don't mention that I just heard her arguing with them outside the door as I was waiting. They want to operate, but she said no. Evidentially she doesn't agree with their diagnosis. She wants more time to work with me. I'm beginning to like this Susan. She looks like a literature professor I once had. Older, petite, beautiful silver hair pulled back in a low ponytail, and warm grey eyes that sparkle when she smiles.

"It's a physical disease caused by calcium deposits in the brain. It can cause hallucinations and depression. It is believed that 1.3 million Americans have it, maybe more. It is very hard to diagnose, and therefore many people don't even know they have it. There are no outward signs except severe headaches and sleepwalking. It usually effects people between the ages of fifty and eighty-five, and there is no known cure, although there has been some success in using antidepressant medications as treatment. Do you think you have Lewy Bodies?"

"I don't know," I say. How the hell should I know? They're the doctors, aren't they?

"Well, I don't," she says. "I think you are suffering from acute post-traumatic stress disorder, delayed. Do you know what that is?"

"Yes, I think so." Why is she treating me like a child? Does she think I'm an idiot? Just because I almost burned a house down doesn't mean I'm stupid.

"I believe there was a traumatic event that occurred in your childhood that you have buried very deep. I want to help you uncover that childhood event, because I believe that will be your cure."

I just nod and smile, although I have my doubts.

"You'll have to trust me, Teresa, and know that I don't want to hurt you or shame you in any way. All I want is to help you to get well. Are you willing?"

I nod again.

"We are going to start by envisioning we are archaeologists on a dig. We are looking for a lost civilization. That civilization is your life, do you understand?

I nod, but I really don't understand what she's talking about.

"I'm going to ask you questions about your childhood, and whenever you start to feel uncomfortable in any way—that's a clue that we've excavated a rare artifact. We will then back up and change our tools from shovels to brushes and proceed very slowly and gently in that area. Do you understand?"

"I guess so," I say. So those are my choices. I either have an incurable disease or I'm crazy.

But wait—I was not hallucinating my own father's picture or handwritten letters. I had physical evidence of these things and I burned them all. Just as I know in my heart and soul that Marina was real and that she is my sister, I really have nothing to show for it. No proof. I want to get well, be normal again, but I also know deep down in my heart that these things really happened to me. It was not all just a dream.

"It's not going to be easy, but just know that it's going to be worth it. Okay?"

"Okay." I'm starting to feel like a child, alone and scared. What would Marina do?

"Good. Let's begin then. Tell me about your earliest memory."

We go on like that for an hour or so. She asks me to tell her my happiest memory, my saddest, and the most confusing memory from my earliest childhood. Then we talk about dreams and I tell her about the reoccurring dreams I have. She never once looks at her watch, and she never once asks me about Marina. She must know about Marina from the other doctors. Maybe she doesn't believe in her, I don't know, but I do know that I'm beginning to trust her for some reason. I don't know why, maybe because she's my only hope. I decide to open up just a little more.

"And every night while lying in bed," I tell her, "I would to listen to my parents arguing. I became so accustomed to it, that if it suddenly got quiet, I would get scared. The arguing became a sort of nighttime lullaby."

Dr. Wilson nods, and I continue:

"Soon, I began to hear voices arguing in my head."

"Ok, let's put a stake here and mark this ground for further exploration. I think that's enough for the day, don't you?"

I'm not tired or even emotional. I could go on, but instead I thank her politely and get up to leave.

"It's a nice evening for a walk on the beach," she says. "You should take one before dinner. It will help clear your mind."

"I think I will. Thank you." And I walk out the door and head to the back stair and down the steps toward the beach.

I'm walking along the sand, thinking about my session with Dr. Wilson. The ocean is rough tonight, slamming against the shore in anger. It takes me back to that little girl lying in bed, listening to my parents arguing. My mother is screaming at my father. I can't hear what she's saying, but I know the words are confusing, and they are making me sad.

That all seems so trivial now in the light of my diagnosis. What difference does it make what kind of childhood I had if I have Lewy Bodies? Why can't we just leave the past alone?

Michael thinks I'm crazy. Poor thing. He doesn't know how to deal with me. He's been walking on eggshells ever since he moved me into this place. But I'm starting to like it here, and my burns are almost all healed now. The doctor says I can have surgery to repair some of the worst scars, but I don't mind really. Scars, like wrinkles, are a sign of a life well-lived, I always say.

I cried when they told me that they couldn't recover that picture of my father. And I cried when Michael told me the parlor had burned to the ground. He wants to open the dining room up to the garden, keep the fireplace, but have it open on both sides, and add French doors that lead out to an outdoor dining terrace. Let the sun in. Yes, it's time to let the sun in. I'm going to miss that room though, but it will always be there, really, just in the open now. I'm going to miss Marina too, but she will always be here as well, I guess.

Can these Lewy Bodies be nature's way of allowing us the ability to communicate with the dead? How did I know things about her nobody else knew? Am I really crazy? Or did this not really happen? And the dreams—they are so real. Maybe Marina had this disease too and that's why she killed herself. Or maybe it was just pure sadness that killed her. That poor girl, growing up without a father, and an alcoholic mother that was all but absent as well. I'm wondering what I would do in that situation. I didn't have the best childhood in the world. I also had no father to be there for me, so I could definitely feel for her. And my mother? I don't really remember her being there for me either. Growing up all alone, with nobody to turn to. And nobody to reassure me that I am worthy, that I am loveable, that I am smart and pretty. A child needs love and reassurance from their parents.

I love walking on the beach. There are so many shells on this beach. Each one a reminder of a life lived. I'll pick up just one shell today, to mark my time in recovery. I'll walk every day on this beach, and each day I'll pick up a shell, like a memory. My own past seems like another life. Several lives, in fact. Maybe I'm starting a new one each day I spend here.

As an adult, I suppose I have to reassure myself, my inner child, that everything's going to be ok, and that I am worthy. I am the only one who can nurture myself now. I know I must do this, somehow. But I don't really know how to nurture myself. I think back to the days when Carly was a little girl. I showered her with praise. I suppose I was trying to compensate for my lost childhood. I remember those long, happy summer afternoons in the park with her. Playing on the swings and singing. We would make up little songs together. We would each take a turn and sing a line, trying to rhyme with the previous line in our little song. What fun we had! I didn't have a care in the world back then, and Carly was such a happy child. I wish I had happy memories like that of my own childhood, but I just can't remember any. In fact, I can't remember much of my childhood at all. Oh yes, bits and pieces I can recall, the bad times mostly. But everyday memories, like the ones I have with Carly? No. I guess I just packed them up and put them away somewhere, like the photos in the bottom drawer of my downstairs cabinet back home in New York.

Maybe something bad did happen to me as a child. I suppose it's a possibility. Well, it's better than having a brain disease anyway.

I want to play again. I want to play and sing and be creative and happy. I don't care what they say I have, or what my childhood was like. I want to write poetry, I want to write songs, make music, paint, create something. My life was almost taken away from me. It's time now to start living it again.

A lone seagull flies overhead, screaming into the wind, crying for its mates. The rest of the flock shows up and now they are all squawking, and diving into the rough surf for their supper. I stand there, watching the scene for a while, then turn and head back to get my own dinner.

Dr. Wilson wants me to start keeping a journal.

"Just write down whatever comes to mind at the time," she said.

I feel the need to write about my changing world and what it's becoming. But it's sometimes too frightening to ponder, and so perhaps my throwback to the fifties is just what I need. Maybe I'll just write about Marina and the dreams she shared with me about her childhood. My own childhood couldn't have been any worse than that. And my future couldn't possibly be as bad as hers was either, could it?

## TWENTY-SIX

"I had another dream about Marina last night."

I'm sitting in Dr. Susan's office, sipping some coffee and talking about whatever comes to mind, my usual morning routine.

"Really? Was it a reoccurring dream or a new one?" she asks.

"Well, it started out like all the others: slipping out of the garden gate on a moonlit night. But instead of walking to the graveyard, she turned right and headed towards the pier." I've told her about all my dreams of Marina and my experiences with her. I think she is the only one who really believes me.

"Go on," she says.

*The moon was high, and the clouds were rolling in fast and low. The wind was fierce, but it wasn't raining. There was electricity in the air. I could see the hairs on the back of her neck stand up. As she walked, she thought about the day's events. Finding the letter from her father, and the confrontation she had with her mother. "How could she have lied to me all those years? How could she make be believe my father died out at sea fighting the enemy during the war, when she knew that my real father was the enemy? And she knew that my real father had in fact killed her husband out at sea that night! How could she watch me suffer with that all those years? Knowing all along that my father wanted to come back into our lives? And why? Why not let him? And why not just tell me the truth?"*

*As she stood at the edge of the pier it occurred to her that her life was over. She could never be happy again. There was just no living with this pain. She opened her arms and lifted her face to the sky as the wind kicked up and lifted her off her feet. For a few seconds, she was flying in the air. She floated with the wind and then dropped into the warm water below. All was peaceful.*

"That was the night Marina died. I don't believe she wanted to kill herself, not really. She was just looking for relief," I tell Dr. Susan.

"Yes, I believe you're right. Suicide is such a permanent solution to what is always a temporary problem. That's why we're here, you and I. It's always best to try to work through our problems, don't you think? Well, I believe that's enough for today."

"Michael's coming to visit. We're going for a picnic on the beach," I say, as I get up to leave.

I've been feeling good lately. Almost myself again. And Michael and I are doing good lately too. He's been busy, finishing the house for me. I can't wait to see it again. The landscaping is in and the pool is finished. He installed the spitter fountains along the sides like I had envisioned all those months ago. He says it adds a nice touch to the atmosphere of the backyard. Maybe they'll let me out soon to go see it. Dr. Susan says I'm not ready to go back to Villa Cheralena just yet. She says my progress is going so well, and she doesn't want to jeopardize it.

I don't know what to believe anymore. It's as if I'm floating in limbo. Just going through the motions. Every day I get up, brush my teeth, go for more tests, have my sessions with Dr. Susan, and go for a walk on the beach. It's all so routine, but it seems like I'm going nowhere. Like a hamster on a slow-motion wheel. If this is progress, I don't see it.

I'm sitting in Dr. Susan's office on a beautiful, sunny day for another one of my regular daily sessions. I'm looking past her wing-back chair at all the shells I've been collecting every morning. One for every day of my recovery. She suggested I put them on her windowsill so I can see how far I've come in my progress. There are dozens of shells, all lined up on the sill now.

"Let's talk about Marina's childhood again now, shall we?" she asks.

"I don't know that much about it, only what she shared with me through my dreams," I say.

"That's fine. The dreams you have been having about Marina's childhood, they must have been some very painful memories for her to share with you. Were they painful for her, do you think?"

"Oh, yes. Very much so. I think that's why she was sharing them. Kind of like what we're doing here. I think she needed to get those memories off her chest, so to speak," I say.

"Yes."

"I think she needed to tell somebody."

"Yes, I believe you're right."

"Tell me about the time Marina was raped on the golf course."

"No, no, she wasn't raped, I told you. She was almost raped. But she saved herself by lying, and telling the boys that she had her period," I say. Doesn't she take notes? How could she not remember that detail?

"Ok. She was almost raped. Tell me about the pile of leaves."

"What do you mean? It was just a pile of leaves. What about them?" I'm getting a little impatient now. Why does she want to know about that? That's such an insignificant little detail. The girl was molested, for God's sake! Who cares about the stupid leaves?

"What kind of leaves were they?"

"I don't know. Whatever kind of leaves grow on golf courses in Florida, I suppose."

"Well? What kind of leaves grow on golf courses in Florida?"

"How the hell should I know?" What is this? She's really annoying me now. She's making me feel guilty, like I've done something wrong. Like I'm trying to hide something from her. Why would I do that? I'm paying her, after all. She works for me. I need to get out of here. I'm getting tired of coming here every morning, and besides I think I'm ready to leave here now. What more could we possibly talk about?

"Teresa."

"What?" I wish I had a cigarette. I'm so annoyed with her right now.

"Try to picture the leaves," she says.

Oh, shut up! I wish she would just shut up right now. She's sitting there all high and mighty in her wing-back chair.

"Teresa," she says again, softly.

"What?" I really wish I had that cigarette. Wait. – I don't smoke. Did Marina smoke? No, Marina never smoked. I was the one who used to smoke. Yes. It was me. I smoked as a teenager. That's right. I quit so long ago; I must have forgotten.

"Picture yourself lying on top of that pile of leaves now. Pretend that you're Marina and you've just been raped—well, almost raped. Now tell me. What kind of leaves do you see?"

"I don't know what kind of leaves, God dammit!" I stand up so abruptly that I knock over the coffee table, spilling my coffee all over her sisal rug, and I storm out of the office.

I'm walking toward the beach now, running really. I can see those leaves clearly in my mind's eye. But I don't want to see those leaves. No, I don't want to see them. The ocean is angry. White foam is pounding onto the shore, and the wind is whipping at my hair.

With each crash of the waves, I see those leaves in my mind's eye; Maple, Oak, Hickory.

They're colored all the shades of fall. No, they are not Florida leaves at all. I'm crying now, crying and running down the beach.

"Help me! Please.... God, help me!"

I fall to my knees in the sand as the waves splash violently over me like the realization itself. Finally, I get up and slowly walk back to Dr. Susan's office, wet and full of sand. She's just sitting there— waiting for me.

"I was thirteen. My father was due to visit that next day, a very rare occasion, and one that I was not looking forward to. I was at the park with some friends that warm autumn evening. One of the boys got a bottle of cheap scotch."

Dr. Susan is just sitting there, not saying a word.

"We were playing a game. A drinking game. We all sat in a circle and one person was handed the bottle of J&B to chug while the others counted out loud. One, two, three…. Whoever got the most counts while chugging down the scotch won. It was my turn next. I put the bottle to my lips. I remember the group counting. I was determined to win this game, wanting so badly to be accepted by this crowd. Joey was there, and I had a crush on him. One, two, three…. I kept on chugging that scotch like it was water. Four, five, six…. I remember the stink of it, and how it burned my throat and all the way down to my stomach. Seven, eight, nine…. I could hear the excitement in their voices, I was sure to win this game and then Joey would like me."

I don't dare look at Dr. Susan, for fear I might chicken out. So, with my eyes cast down, focusing on the coffee stain on the sisal rug, I continue:

"The next thing I knew I was lying in a pile of leaves. Everyone was gone. I knew something bad had happened, and that I was to blame. I remember lying there with leaves in my hair and underpants, just wanting to die."

Tears are slowly slipping from my eyes, and I feel a hundred miles away from reality. I look out, past the picture window, to the sea.

"When I came to, I was in my bed at home. I could hear my parents' hushed voices just outside my door. Then my father walked into my room and sat on the edge of my bed. "When I walk you down the aisle, I want to be proud of you", was all he said, and then he walked out and shut the door behind him. I lay there all alone feeling bewildered and ashamed for something I must have done but couldn't for the life of me remember. I heard them arguing in the dining room. I heard the clanging of silverware on plates. They were having dinner. I must have lost the entire day. What were they fighting about? I strained to listen. I was so used to hearing them fight, it seemed normal. But now my mother was crying, screaming really.

"Why don't you just go back to her? Go back to your lover and that illegitimate daughter that you love so much! I know that you never loved me, that you never loved your real daughter. Only them! You only loved them! Why didn't you go back to them, then? I know why, because they wouldn't have you either, would they? Go on, get out of here, you bastard, and never come back! This is all your fault! If Teresa had a father, this never would have happened!"

"I looked outside my window and noticed it was dark. The entire day had gone by and I couldn't remember anything, but I knew I was in trouble. I must have passed out again, because the next thing I remember, it was morning, and my mother was standing over me with a glass of orange juice."

Dr. Susan gets up and pours me a glass of water and places it on the coffee table in front of me. She doesn't say a word.

"She told me I had come home, half-dressed and filthy dirty, and so drunk she thought I was going to die. She told me she had taken me to the hospital to pump my stomach, but it was too late. The alcohol was already in my bloodstream. They kept me in the hospital overnight for observation, just to make sure I didn't die of alcohol poisoning.

"Evidently, I had been cursing at the doctors and nurses and my mother was ashamed of my behavior. I was grounded for a month, and I was to never use such foul language again! "How could I do this to her? And on the day my father was visiting. I should be ashamed!"

Finally, Dr. Susan speaks up: "Did your mother ever ask you who did that to you, or even what happened?"

"No," I say.

"Surely, she must have known you were molested."

"She never even asked me if I was ok. In fact, we never spoke of it again."

"Who could let this happen to a young girl, and not try to find the person responsible, not press charges? You know this was not your fault, right?"

"I guess I realize in my head that it wasn't, but that little girl inside of me doesn't know that."

"That poor little girl, my heart goes out to her. I want to heal her and make her well again," Dr. Susan says.

"The memories are still so painful, that it helps for me to believe that it didn't really happen to me, but to some other girl."

"Ah, Marina."

"I had blocked it out of my memory for so long. I don't know."

"Do you think that maybe you invented Marina so she could shoulder this burden you've been carrying for so long?"

"I don't know anymore."

"I think that's enough for today. You did good, Teresa. We had a real breakthrough. I believe you're going to fully recover. Why don't you go write in your journal now, and then maybe you'll want to take a nice stroll along the beach again tonight."

It's all coming back to me now, as I open my journal the floodgates of my lost memory have suddenly opened.

I was the one who was abandoned by my father. I was the one who had an alcoholic mother who was never there, and yes, I was the one who was on that golf course on that warm autumn night, all those years ago.

And I was the one who was gang raped by those boys from school.

They were holding my arms, Joey and Stevie, and laughing while Billy pulled his pants down and got on top of me. 'You've been asking for this, you little whore,' he said. He smelled of

257

whiskey and marijuana as he put his hand over my mouth. He told me if I didn't stop screaming, he would kill me. He pulled up my new white skirt, and with his filthy hands he ripped off my underpants, and then he took my innocence. I was terrified and ashamed all at once. I wished I could pass out and not remember what was happening to me. I stopped struggling and shut my eyes tight, hoping it would end soon. Wishing he would just kill me, praying for it to be over. Then he got off me and Joey was next, and then Stevie and the other boy. I thought it was never going to end. And when they were finished, they just left me there on that pile of leaves, all torn and bleeding, but I did not cry. Somehow the pain was a comfort to my shame. I was numb to all feelings as I lay there, very still, waiting to die.

I promised myself never to tell a soul about what happened. I felt dirty and responsible, guilty and ashamed. I never saw those boys again. By the grace of God, that fall we moved, and by Christmas I was enrolled in a new high school where nobody knew me. I was able to start fresh. I learned how to reinvent myself. I pushed that memory, along with all the other painful memories, into the black hole that was somewhere beyond the reach of my consciousness. I never thought of it again, until it no longer happened to me. If it happened at all, it happened to someone else.

I close my Journal and put down my pen.

The evening sun is warm on my shoulders and the tide is going out now as I walk slowly along the beach. The waves have subsided, and they hit the shore like a mother's sigh.

## TWENTY-SEVEN

All those painful memories I tried so hard to hide all my adult life—I stuffed them down so deep, nobody alive could ever find them. Marina came to help me. She knew they were there. Marina came to show me that I was not alone. That I am not the only little girl who was abandoned and abused as a child. While I have been restoring her house, Marina has been restoring my childhood. But is she for real?

Who is Marina? Is she the daughter my father wanted? The little girl my father loved? Or is she just some girl who drowned in the water during a storm.

I'm looking at the page I just wrote in my journal and noticing bits and pieces of my life coming back to me. As if a floodgate has opened, suddenly I am remembering my painful childhood. Painful memories I had pushed deep down. Evicted from my brain, they have come back to haunt me. Just like matter, memories never die—they change into calcium deposits and cling onto the outskirts of the brain like neglected children, trying to get in. Fighting to be restored.

I'm writing down my story every night, and in doing so I am renovating my very soul. Just like Villa Cheralena, though I first had to tear down the old walls, filled with black mold, before I could begin my restoration. Dr. Wilson says the writing is doing me good. She says our sessions are going well, and that I am going to fully recover. Every day I walk on the beach after our session, and every night I write about my life. Perhaps I'll turn this into a book and get it published, so other people like me can also see they are not alone.

Michael came to see me again today. We talked about the renovation. It's coming along nicely, he says. They are installing the new pecky cypress tongue-and-groove ceiling in the dining room. The furniture is going to be delivered next week. Turns out, it was the original table and chairs from the house. I knew that dining room set belonged there. They opened the dining room to the garden beyond and Michael says it really looks great. There are new French doors flanking the fireplace, and a covered patio just outside, in my secret garden. He bought some outdoor tables and chairs, not unlike the ones at my favorite café, The Patio. He also added an outdoor fireplace, against the one in the dining room, so you can sit out there by the fire and look at the pool. It sounds nice. I'm glad he's going ahead with the restorations. I can't wait to see it finished.

He said they're letting me out of here soon. He's been such a good husband, and a good friend. I love him very much. He quit his job and moved into the master suite as soon as it was finished.

He asked me if we should sell now that the house is finished. He thinks I won't be able to handle living there, with all the memories. But I feel just the opposite. I wouldn't want to live anywhere else.

Lucy came to see me as well. We chatted a bit, mostly small talk. I asked her about Daisy and Agnus, how they are doing. Daisy went out to California to visit some distant relatives. She might be staying there indefinitely, Lucy says. And Agnus is doing fine, she sends her love, says she misses me and hopes for a speedy recovery. We never mentioned Marina. I'm not sure if people think I'm crazy, or if they believe I really did see her. I leave it alone, unsure of what to think myself.

I've decided to rename the house "Casa Marina." It seems fitting, and the least I can do for her. This is her house, after all. Even if I was imagining her ghost all along, the fact remains that she did exist, and she would have been the rightful owner of this house after her mother died, if she had survived.

## TWENTY-EIGHT

A young girl in a pink jacket, rows her long white boat all alone, through the still, early morning waters. The only movement I can see are her oars dipping into the water to some universal rhythm, and the ripples caused by the bow of the boat as it slices silently through. They form a V at the bow and spread out, ever widening. The sun is rising in the eastern sky, throwing rays upward through the magenta clouds. A solitary soul glides through the water. Birds sing in the trees. The whole planet rejoices at the break of a new day.

And me, as I sit on my rocking chair on the new deck of the third-floor observation room, coffee in hand, a witness to the beauty of it all. A new beginning. Gratitude fills my heart as tears fill my eyes. I get to have another chance; to start anew. She never had that chance, my poor little big sister. I say a prayer for her.

What does it all mean, this life we're thrown into? All we humans ever really want is to be loved by someone, to be wanted. To have a purpose in someone else's life. To be significant. I guess that is meaning enough for me today. Marina couldn't find that while she was alive on this earth, but she helped me find it, and I hope she too has found it now. I know no one believes my incredible story about how Marina came back to haunt me, but it's ok.

Another rower comes by on his boat. Maybe he's looking for the girl in the pink jacket. I look out over the water, the island beyond, and the ocean beyond that, and wonder about their lives.

Some cars drive by now, going north on Flagler, probably headed to Palm Beach. The world around me is waking up and people are starting their day. I hear my husband out front talking to Carly. Thoughts of Marina, and my own sense of solitude slowly slip away.

There's a tap at the door and Agnus walks out and sits down next to me. I wonder how this old woman climbed all the way up those stairs.

"Good morning to you," she says with a sly smile.

"Good morning to you!" I say. "How the hell did you get up here? And why didn't you tell Michael to come and get me, I would have come down."

"I wanted to be alone with you for a while. I have something to give you. And besides, I wanted to see this view one more time before I die."

She hands me an envelope. I open it and pull out an old photograph. It's a picture of me. No. It's a picture of Marina. It looks like her high school yearbook photo. On the back is written: "Dear Nissy, I'll always love you, Marina.

"Oh, Agnus, I couldn't—"

"Please. I want you to have it. I don't need any proof; I know she was real. But someday you just might be questioning, and well, I thought it might come as a handy reminder that you're not crazy."

"Oh, Agnus. Thank you so much. You're coming to the party tomorrow, right?"

"Of course, I am, honey. I wouldn't miss it for the world."

Tomorrow is our Grand Opening and the place is booked through the season. I know it's going to be a big success. Michael's here, Carly's here, Agnus is here, and somewhere in my heart, I know Marina's here too.

The End

Made in USA - North Chelmsford, MA
21823_9798387313905
10.23.2023 0529